THE PHANTOM AMBUSHED
IN A SHEIK'S HAREM?

There was no immediate escape route. Without hesitation, he spread his arms so that they touched three or four girls on either side, and moved rapidly to the pool. A half dozen girls ahead were propelled with them as he jumped into the pool, pulling them all with him.

There was pandemonium in the harem as the others ran every which way screaming .... the amazed soldiers ran to the edge of the pool, trying to spot the big stranger whom they had glimpsed only briefly. He wasn't in sight. He was somewhere underwater, among the trashing bodies.

Hermes Press

Published by Hermes Press, an imprint of Herman and Geer Communications, Inc.
Daniel Herman, Publisher
Troy Musguire, Production Manager
Eileen Sabrina Herman, Managing Editor
Alissa Fisher, Graphic Design
Kandice Hartner, Senior Editor
Benjamin Beers, Archivist

2100 Wilmington Road
Neshannock, Pennsylvania, 16105
(724) 652-0511
www.HermesPress.com; info@hermespress.com

Cover image: Painting of The Phantom by George Wilson
Book design by Eileen Sabrina Herman
First printing, 2020

LCCN applied for: 0 1 2 3 4 5 6 7 8 9 10
ISBN 978-1-61345-194-6
OCR and text editing by H + G Media and Eileen Sabrina Herman
Proof reading by Eileen Sabrina Herman and Kandice Hartner

From Dan, Louise, Sabrina, Ruckus, and Noodle for D'zur and Mellow

Acknowledgements: This book would not be possible without the help, cooperation, patience, and kindness of many people. First and foremost in making this endeavor a reality are Ita Golzman and Frank Caruso at King Features. Thanks also to Pete Klaus and the late Ed Rhoades of "The Friends of the Phantom." Pete and Ed have provided us with resource material, contacts, information, and helpful insights into the strip and continue to be there when we have questions about the world of The Ghost Who Walks.

Editor's Note: There were several misspellings in the original text; those have been corrected with this reprint. However, the alternate spelling for the Singh pirates as Singg was kept to preserve the original format.

Printed in Canada

AUTHORS NOTE

Old friends of the PHANTOM adventure strip may be interested to know more about this series of novels with the general title, The Story of the Phantom.

All are based on my original stories. I wrote *They Story of the Phantom—The Ghost Who Walks, The Mysterious Ambassador, Killer's Town, The Vampires and the Witch*, and this book, *The Curse of the Two-Headed Bull*.

Basil Copper adapted *The Slave Market of Mucar*, and *The Scorpia Menace*. Frank S. Shawn adapted *The Veiled Lady, The Golden Circle, The Hydra Monster, The Mystery of the Sea Horse, The Goggle-Eyes Pirates*, and *The Swamp Rats*. Warren Shanahan adapted *The Island of Dogs*, and Carson Bingham adapted *The Assassins*.

The Story of THE PHANTOM and
The Curse of the Two-Headed Bull

Lee Falk

CONTENTS

WITH THE PHANTOM, EVERYTHING IS POSSIBLE— EXCEPT BOREDOM

by
Francis Lacassin, Lecturer
The Sorbonne, Paris, France

When Lee Falk introduced into comic-strip format the imaginary and the fantastic with the figure of *Mandrake, The Magician*, it was apparent that he was contributing to what I describe to my students at the Sorbonne as "The Ninth Art." It was even more evident when he invented The Phantom, a figure who set the fashion for the masked and costumed Man of Justice,

On November 15, 1971, the oldest university in Europe, the Sorbonne, opened its doors to the comics. I was privileged to give, with the section of Graphic Arts, a weekly two-hour course in the History of the Aesthetics and Language of Comic Strips. Prior sessions had been devoted to the *Phantom*. The female students were drawn to the attractiveness and elegance of his figure; the men liked his masculinity and humor. To me, Lee Falk's stories—representing as they do the present-day *Thousand and One Nights*, fairy tales, *The Tales of the Knights of the Round Table*, etc.—adapt the epic poetry for the dreams and needs of an advanced and industrial civilization. For me the Phantom reincarnates Achilles, the valorous warrior of the Trojan War, and like a knight he wanders about the world in search of a crime to castigate or a wrong to right.

Lee Falk's art of storytelling is defined as much by the succinctness of the action, as by that of the dialogue. The text has not only a dry, terse quality, but also delicious humor. The humor shows itself in the action by the choice of daring ellipses: nothing remains but the strong points of the action. This allows the story to progress more rapidly and reduces the gestures of the hero to those which underlie his fantastic physical prowess. Falk gives the drama in a nutshell. A remarkable example is the resume done in four frames (in the comic strip) and placed at the beginning of each episode to recall the Phantom's origins. In four pictures, everything about the man is said, his romantic legend, his noble mission. Moreover, the new reader enters the fabulous world of Lee Falk, where nothing is real but everything is possible—except boredom.

Dressed in a soft hat and an overcoat with the collar upturned, the Phantom and his wolf, Devil, wander about the world, the cities of Europe, or, dressed in his eighteenth-century executioner's costume, he passes his time in the jungle. Wherever he is, he acts like a sorcerer of the fantastic. Under his touch, the real seems to crack and dreams well through.

A masked ball in the Latin Quarter appears. In the Phantom's eyes it is the rendezvous of a redoubtable secret society of women. The jungle vegetation becomes the jewel box in which are hidden lost cities, sleeping gods, vampire queens, tournaments worthy of the Olympic Games. The geography, the flowers, the animals in their turn undergo a magical change brought on by the hero. A savage continent borders the edge of the Deep Woods. It is protected by a praetorian guard, the pygmies. The Skull Cave contains the treasures of war and the archives of his ancestors. All this occurs on a mythical continent which is not exactly Africa nor exactly Asia, because the tigers and lions are friends.

The genius of Lee Falk is to have known how to create a new *Odyssey*, with all of its fantastic color, but what is even more surprising is that it would be believable in the familiar settings of the modern world. The Phantom acts with the audacity of Ulysses and also with the nobility of a knight-errant. In contrast to Ulysses, and similarly to Sir Lancelot, he moves about in the world of his own free will among his peers. Lee Falk has not only managed to combine epic poetry with fairy tales and the stories of chivalry, he has made of the Phantom, in a jungle spared by colonialism, an agent of political equilibrium and friendship between races. In giving his hero an eternal mission, Lee Falk has made him so real, so near, so believable that he has made of him a man of all times. He will outlive him as Ulysses has outlived Homer. But in contrast to Ulysses, his adventures will continue after his creator is gone, because his creator has made of him an indispensable figure endowed with a life of his own. This is a privilege of which the heroes of written word cannot partake; no one has been able to imitate Homer.

However, the comic strip is the victim of a fragile medium, the newspaper. Because of this, some adventures of *The Phantom* have been lost and live only in the memory of their readers. This memory is difficult to communicate to others. Lee Falk has, therefore, given a new dimension to *The Phantom* by making of him the hero of a series of novels, introducing his origins and his first adventures to those who did not know him before.

This is not his least important accomplishment, but the most significant in my opinion is this: —in presenting to us The Phantom, as a friend, Lee Falk has taught us to dream, which is something no school in the world can teach.

Francis Lacassin
June, 1972
Paris

PROLOGUE

How It All Began

*O*ver *four hundred years ago, a large British merchant ship was attacked by Singg pirates off the remote shores of Bangalla. The captain of the trading vessel was a famous seafarer who, in his youth, had served as cabin boy to Christopher Columbus on his first voyage to discover the New World. With the captain was his son, Kit, a strong young man who idolized his father and hoped to follow him as a seafarer. But the pirate attack was disastrous. In a furious battle, the entire crew of the merchant ship was killed and the ship sank in flames. The sole survivor was young Kit who, as he fell off the burning ship, saw his father killed by a pirate. Kit was washed ashore, half-dead. Friendly pygmies found him and nursed him to health.*

One day, walking on the beach, he found a dead pirate dressed in his fathers clothes. He realized this was the pirate who had killed his father. Grief-stricken, he waited until vultures had stripped the body clean. Then on the skull of his father's murderer, he swore an oath by firelight as the pygmies watched. "I swear to devote my life to the destruction of piracy, greed, cruelty, and injustice – and my sons and their sons shall follow me."

This was the Oath of the Skull that Kit and his descendants would live by. In time, the pygmies led him to their home in the Deep Woods in the center of the jungle, where he found a large cave with many rocky chambers. The mouth of the cave, a natural formation formed by the water and wind of centuries, was curiously like a skull. This became his home, the Skull Cave. He soon adopted a mask and a strange costume. He found that the mystery and fear this inspired helped him in his endless battle against world-wide piracy. For he and his sons who followed became known as the nemesis of pirates everywhere, a mysterious man whose face no one ever saw, whose name no one knew, who worked alone.

As the years passed, he fought injustice wherever he found it. The first Phantom and the sons who followed found their wives in many places. One married a reigning queen, one a princess, one a beautiful red-haired barmaid. But whether queen or commoner, all followed their men back to the Deep Woods to live the strange but happy life of the wife of the Phantom. And of all the world, only she, wife of the Phantom and their children, could see his face.

Generation after generation was conceived and born, grew to manhood, and assumed the tasks of the father before him. Each wore the mask and costume. Folk of the jungle and the city and sea began to whisper that there was a man who could not die, a Phantom, a Ghost Who Walks. For they thought the Phantom was always the same man. A boy who saw the Phantom would see him again fifty years after; and he seemed the same. And he would tell his son and his grandson; and then his son and grandson would see the Phantom fifty years after that. And he would seem the same. So the legend grew. The Man Who Cannot Die. The Ghost Who Walks. The Phantom.

The Phantom did not discourage this belief in his immortality. Always working alone against tremendous – sometimes almost impossible – odds, he found that the awe and fear the legend inspired was a great help in his endless battle against evil. Only his friends, the pygmies, knew the truth. To compensate for their tiny stature, the pygmies, mixed deadly poisons for use on their weapons in hunting or defending themselves. It was rare that they were forced to defend themselves. Their deadly poisons were known through the jungle, and they and their home, the Deep Woods, were dreaded and avoided. Another reason to stay away from the Deep Woods – it soon became known that this was a home of the Phantom, and none wished to trespass.

Through the ages, the Phantoms created several more homes, or hideouts, in various parts of the world. Near the Deep Woods was the Isle of Eden, where the Phantom taught all animals to live in peace. In the southwest desert of the New World, the Phantoms created an eyrie on a high, steep mesa that was thought by the Indians to be haunted by evil spirits and became known as "Walker's Table" – for the Ghost Who Walks. In Europe, deep in the crumbling cellars of ancient castle ruins, the Phantom had another hideout from which to strike against evildoers.

But the Skull Cave in the quiet of the Deep Woods remained the true home of the Phantom. Here, in a rocky chamber, he kept his chronicles, written records of all his adventures. Phantom after Phantom faithfully recorded their experiences in the large folio volumes. Another chamber contained the costumes of all the generations of Phantoms. Other chambers contained the vast treasures of the Phantom acquired over the centuries, used only in the endless battle against evil.

Thus twenty generations of Phantoms lived, fought, and died, usually violently, as they fulfilled their oath. Jungle folk, sea folk and city folk believed him the same man, the Man Who Cannot Die. Only the pygmies knew that always, a day would come when their great friend would die. Then, alone, a strong young son would carry his father to the burial crypt of his ancestors where all Phantoms rested. As the pygmies waited outside, the young man would emerge from the cave, wearing the mask, the costume, and the skull ring of the Phantom; his carefree, happy days as the Phantom's son were over. And the pygmies would chant their age-old chant, "The Phantom is dead. Long live the Phantom."

The story of the Island of Dogs is an adventure of the Phantom of our time—the twenty-first generation of his line. He has inherited the traditions and responsibilities created by four centuries of Phantom ancestors. One ancestor created the Jungle Patrol. Thus, today, our Phantom is the mysterious and unknown commander of this elite corps. In the jungle, he is known and loved as The Keeper of the Peace. On his right hand is the Skull Ring that leaves his mark— the Sign of the Skull—known and feared by evildoers everywhere. On his left hand—closer to the heart—is his "good mark" ring. Once given, the mark grants the lucky bearer protection by the Phantom, and it is equally known and respected. And to good people and criminals alike in the jungle, on the seven seas, and in the cities of the world he is the Phantom, the Ghost Who Walks, the Man Who Cannot Die.

Lee Falk
New York 1973

CHAPTER 1

If you were on the beach that sunny afternoon, you'd have seen an unusual sight. Two full-grown jungle cats, a Bengal tiger and an African lion, galloping shoulder to shoulder like circus animals on the sand. Standing on their backs, one foot on each huge beast, balancing like a circus rider to remain upright, was a tall man clad only in a loincloth. His skin was bronze from the sun, and his body might have been carved by Michelangelo, so perfect were the proportions of his powerful physique. Thundering behind like children following a circus parade was an odd mixture of animals—a giraffe, a leopard, a zebra, a black panther, several varieties of antelope, an elephant, a gorilla. Watching them, you'd have the impression they'd shout and laugh like children if they could. If you looked at the lagoon next to the beach, you would see two large dolphins leaping through the shallow water, keeping up with the parade. Beyond the lagoon and the sharp coral reefs that protected it from the open sea, you might have noticed a body floating on the gentle waves.

The man, busy keeping his balance on his galloping mounts, had not seen it yet. For he was no circus rider, and these were not circus animals. None of them, with the exception of the gorilla, had ever seen a cage. The man was the Phantom, the Ghost Who Walks, and the animals were his pets, living on his Isle of Eden.

When the Phantom wanted to get away from it all, he often came to this remote little island. Eden is separated from the jungle by a broad river filled with piranha. These voracious fish, known to strip a full-grown steer down to bones in minutes, protect Eden from jungle animals, and keep the island animals from crossing as well. On the ocean side, coral reefs keep ships and swimmers, fish or mammals, from the island.

Getting away from it all meant leaving the jungle proper and his home in his Skull Cave in the Deep Woods which was also home to his friends, the Bandar, the dreaded pygmy poison people; getting away from the many responsibilities placed upon him by the jungle tribes and twenty generations of Phantom ancestors. Among his duties were: Keeper of the Peace (it is said that in Phantom country, a beautiful woman clad only in jewels could walk the dark paths at midnight without fear); Arbitrator of Argumentation (this covered property disputes, water-rights disputes, stolen goods, lovers' quarrels, wagers, territorial rights, etc.); Guardian of the Eastern Dark (this referred back to olden times of slavery, when cruel slavers invaded the jungle from the Misty Mountains to the east). In addition, the Phantom attended chiefs' parleys, manhood initiation rites, weddings ("kiss the bride" . . . "my pleasure"), births ("brings the baby good luck") and funerals. Added to all that, his role as unknown Commander of the far-flung Jungle Patrol. It is no wonder that often, as on this day, he sought the quiet and seclusion of Eden.

The gallop ended when the Phantom lost his balance and somersaulted onto the sand. The lion and tiger nuzzled him happily, and were rewarded with petting; then they turned into the water, as the other animals crowded about their master, whistling, grunting, braying and coughing their delight. He petted each in turn, calling each by name (Baldy the gorilla. Stretch the giraffe, etc.), then followed the great cats into the water to cool off. The lion and tiger had gone to have lunch. The lagoon was heavily stocked with fish of all sizes, from fingerlings to twenty- or thirty-pound sea bass. From the time they had been kittens, he had raised all the cats on fish, gradually teaching them to catch their own. None of them had ever tasted warm-blooded meat, so they could live in peace with the grass-eaters, their normal prey. The lagoon was kept stocked with live fish by the Mori fisherfolk, old friends of the Phantom.

As he swam lazily, fish veered toward him, then flashed away. As soon as the cats caught their lunch and returned to the sand to eat, the huge dolphins leaped through the shallows toward their master. They always waited until the cats left the water, never trusting them. They nuzzled him gently from either side,

Solomon (the wise) and Nefertiti (the beautiful). He stroked them. They persisted in their nuzzling, and he knew what they wanted. He went to a tree near the beach where leather straps and a knife hung from a bough. Returning to the water, he placed a harness over each dolphin's head. In a moment, they were off, leaping at high speed, while he hung on behind, holding onto the reins, waterskiing over the surface on his bare feet—a difficult trick performed only by experienced waterskiers. The dolphins loved this game and headed toward the coral reef which barely broke the surface. When they reached it, they leaped into the air over it. The Phantom, following, dove headlong over the reef, clearing the sharp edges by inches, then regained his stance behind the plunging dolphins as they headed into the open sea. It was exciting sport, touched with the danger that intrigued all jungle folk.

Free of the shallow lagoon, the dolphins raced at top speed—thirty or forty land miles an hour. The water was cooler out here, the waves higher, and the Phantom thrilled to the speed and spray. Suddenly, the dolphins stopped, so suddenly that he pitched forward, almost landing on them. They looked at him, then circled slowly. He knew what that meant. Something nearby—probably a shark.

He looked about quickly. Yes, indeed. Several sinister fins, like small dark sails over the surface. He had brought the knife along for just such a possibility. However, with the dolphins, he had little fear of sharks. It was the other way around. Of all the creatures of the sea, the one sharks probably fear most are dolphins. Dolphins are faster and smarter than the slow-moving, myopic shark. Perhaps there's some ancient enmity between these smart mammals of the sea and the prehistoric, cartilaginous beast called shark. Observers tell us the dolphin leaps about the shark like a relentless fury, hitting him hard, one side, then the other, rupturing the shark, butting him to death.

He dropped the reins. Solomon and Nefertiti moved in slow, wide circles toward the moving fins. Then he saw something floating just beyond the sharks. A form—human —bobbing on the waves. Man or woman, adult or child, he couldn't tell. Alive or dead? He swam toward it, knife in hand.

There was sudden foamy churning to his left. Solomon had reached a shark. For a moment, a twenty-foot man-eater was visible at the surface as Solomon banged into him like a battering ram. Then both moved out of sight. To the right, closer, Nefertiti leaped above the surface in an arc, then landed snout-first below another fin. He could hear that encounter. A wham—like a fist pounded into a palm. Both sank out of sight. He swam on toward the floating figure. A third fin was near it. He took a deep breath and dove deep in its direction. The shark was a whopper—another twenty-footer. It was nosing about close to a trousered leg that dangled below the surface. A man. One snap of those great jaws could remove that leg as cleanly as a surgeon's scalpel. Sensing his approach, the shark turned toward him. He was now beneath the monster. He sliced his knife deep into the gray belly above him, near the heart. Blood poured from the wound, staining the water. Now there was no time to lose. He knew what would happen next.

He popped to the surface beside the floating man, grabbed an arm, and swam away as fast as he could, pulling the man with him. There was something tangled around the arm, a strap attached to a bulky yellow object. No time to stop for a look now. The shark, fatally wounded, was thrashing about, still searching for his prey while his cold life's blood poured from hips. As the Phantom moved away as fast as possible with his burden, another shark brushed past him. The rough filelike sharkskin scraped his leg, but the beast gave no heed to him, so intent was it on reaching its wounded fellow. Whether or not this was one of the sharks attacked by the dolphins, he didn't know. He did know that other sharks would join it rapidly in a mad orgy of eating. They'd be drawn by the taste of blood spreading through the water.

Sharks go crazy with the taste or scent of blood, and this is what was happening now. Several sharks were chomping at their wounded but still living fellow, churning the water, leaping and bouncing against each other in their frenzy to get at the meat. The Phantom swam on as fast as he could. The crazed sharks might turn on him at any moment. He felt a soft body brush him. Not rough sharkhide that could rip like teeth, but sleek and smooth. Nefertiti! He grabbed the trailing rein and, in a moment, was being dragged across the water at high speed, still clinging to the man. Solomon joined, circling and leaping over him, guarding against further shark attack.

Reaching the reef, the dolphins leaped over it. He dropped the reins, and carefully, slowly climbed over the sharp coral with his burden. He paused on the rocks to look at him. The man seemed to be dead . . . but were his lips trembling? The Phantom continued over the rocks into the lagoon. For behind in the open sea, he could still see the hungry sharks at their mad feast. As he moved through the shallow lagoon, he now saw what was tangled on the man's arm. A yellow canvas vest, the sort usually carried on boats.

He waded toward the beach with the man lying limply in his arms. The dolphins leaped behind him, fish swam between his legs, and on shore the animals waited. Until now, he hadn't had a good look at the man's face. It was a face he'd seen before—Old

Murph.

As he placed the old man carefully on the sand, the animals crowded around to see what plaything he'd brought them. He waved them away and searched for signs of life —a heartbeat, respiration. The signs were there, faintly. The lips barely moved, the eyelids fluttered open for a second. His eyes were unfocused. He was trying to say something. The Phantom bent close to his lips.

"Damn thing . . . damn thing . . . true. . . true . . . how you like that. . ."

The voice trailed off. The old man sighed. His eyes seemed to glaze. His breathing and his heart stopped simultaneously. The Phantom instantly started mouth-to-mouth resuscitation, then artificial respiration. It was too late.

The Phantom had seen him several times in the past years. He was a character, well known to the tribes and well liked. In his younger days, he had managed a small trading post, and went from village to village, bartering goods. Later, he served as a guide and translator for visitors from the outside. He always drank too much, but had a reputation for honesty and fair dealing. What had brought him to this remote beach to breath his last?

He showed little sign of exposure to the sea and sun. Evidently, he hadn't been in the water long. What had killed him? Heart failure? Shock? Amazing that the sharks hadn't gotten to him in that infested water. This was more amazing, when in briefly examining the body, the Phantom found the cause of death. Two wounds in the area of the heart. Two parallel holes, small and deep. Apparently, this was murder.

As he sat back to think, a fawn pressed its soft nose against his shoulder. The Phantom stroked him. Who would have killed Old Murph? He was a harmless, likable fellow, not one to get into scrapes, and never had enough money to attract trouble. Had some desperate mugger attacked him on a dark wharf, then pushed him into the water? Had the old man grasped a discarded lifebelt floating in the harbor flotsam? Not likely. The closest coastal town was several hundred miles away. Perhaps the life vest, the sort known as a "Mae West," could help. It did. A faded stencil on the back read: S. S. *Moru Benga*.

Moru Benga. A freighter that carried goods from Mawitaan to other seaports along the coast. He had seen it that very morning at dawn, passing about ten miles away.

He had watched it through a powerful telescope until it disappeared over the horizon. That explained it. Old Murph had only been in the water for a few hours. It should be simple to find out who aboard the *Moru Benga* had stabbed him with an ice pick or some similar weapon. The Jungle Patrol could follow through on the case, but a nagging little feeling told him it wasn't going to be that simple. Not simple at all.

Now, what to do with the remains of Old Murph? Burial was the obvious thing. But not at Eden. The animals were alone most of the time. He couldn't take a chance on the cats digging him up. There were the piranha. They'd make quick work of Murph. He dismissed the thought. No, the old man deserved a dignified burial. Burial at sea. The Mori fishermen were due at twilight, bringing a fresh supply of fish for the lagoon. There were sails from a small catboat he used occasionally.

The Mori war canoe arrived on schedule, manned by six husky fishermen, dragging in its wake a net filled with flopping fish. The catch was dumped into the lagoon. Now, the Phantom was no longer in a loincloth, but clad in his familiar hood and mask outfit. He explained the mission to the men, one that was not new to them. They sewed the body inside the canvas with rock for ballast, using netline. Then the Phantom went with them in the war canoe, out the mouth of the piranha-filled river, moving carefully in a hidden channel through the coral that only the Mori knew, and out into the sea.

They were near the battleground of the sharks. None were in sight. He murmured a brief prayer over the canvas sack, then it was lowered over the side and sank rapidly. He hoped the sharks would not find Old Murph, but if they did . . . he sighed philosophically. He was a jungleman, and he knew all life returned eventually to the sea.

The Mori brought him back to land, but he did not return to Eden. He had planned a few more days there, but the death of Old Murph bothered him. He would get in touch with the Jungle Patrol, have them contact the *Moru Benga* and get to the bottom of this. But the same nagging little feeling remained. It wasn't going to be easy. Somehow, they wouldn't get to the bottom of it just like that. There was more to this than met the eye.

"Damn thing . . . damn thing . . . true . . . true . . . how you like that . . ." Murph's dying words. What did they mean?

CHAPTER 2

He heard the startling news as he galloped through the shadowy jungle trail on Hero, his great white stallion. As usual, Devil, the gray mountain wolf, ran alongside, his pale blue eyes glancing from side to side, alert for any sudden danger. The news came through the jungle stillness via throbbing tom-tom beats. Such news passed from tribe to tribe, picked up and relayed by a variety of drums, tiny and treble, big and bass. Heard from this distance, the orchestra of many drums sounded like a chorus of insects at night. He reined Hero to a stop, so that he could hear more clearly. There was no mistaking the message. The sacred image of the Llongo had disappeared. Stolen.

This was a shocker. He had known about the Llongo sacred image all his life. So had the rest of the jungle folk. It seemed as eternal as the Misty Mountains. It had always been there. Llongo tradition held that the unique object was a gift of the Queen of Sheba to King Solomon. The son of their royal union, tradition also held, had founded the Llongo nation and brought the sacred object with him when his father died. The jungle firmly believed this legend. Not only was the sacred object obviously ancient and magnificent, it also had a special attribute—luck.

"Lucky as a Llongo" was an old jungle saying. "Luck of the Llongo" was a fact. The Wambesi people were richer, with their vast herds. The Oogaan were more gifted, with their brilliant carvings and crafts. The Mori were bolder, the Tirangi fiercer, the Sezami smarter. But the Llongo were the luckiest.

A storm might destroy the nets and boats of the Mori, sweep through the Wambesi fields playing havoc with crops and cattle, destroy Oogaan huts. But always, it seemed, the storm passed harmlessly over the Llongo. Floods might engulf the neighboring Sezami. The Llongo remained dry. Wild elephants might stampede the Wambesi fields; jungle cats might massacre a herd. The Llongo pigs and goats remained untouched.

In games of chance, it was even more obvious. You played cards or dice with a Llongo at your peril. They always won. Bookies at the Mawitaan race track turned pale when the Llongo came to town. Same reason. Let the word get around that a Llongo had bet on a long shot, and the odds dropped at once because he usually won. In all games, this held true. Even in Bingo (a game introduced by the white missionaries). Never bet against a Llongo.

It followed that they always won the prettiest girls. After many generations of this, the Llongo men were the handsomest, their wives the most beautiful, of all jungle people. The Llongo, and the rest of the jungle, attributed all this good luck to their sacred image.

As he rode through the jungle, the quiet broken only by the distant drums, the Phantom recalled the last time he had seen the image. About three months earlier, he had made a ceremonial visit. The occasion was the birth of a son to the beautiful eighteen-year-old bride of the eighty-five-year-old High Chief Llionto. More Llongo luck. After admiring the handsome baby and wading through a gargantuan feast, he strolled with Llionto to look at the sacred image. And once again, the High Chief told him the legend of Solomon and Sheba.

The image was on an altar under a frond-covered roof, open on four sides. A ceremonial guard remained on duty day and night. Though he had seen it before, it was always breathtaking. It was glittering, beautiful. The body was about two feet long. There was a lowered head at each end, sprouting long curving horns. The body was made of deep green jade, inset with massive emeralds, diamonds and rubies. Golden strands coiled about the jewels and sharp horns. In bright sunlight, it was so brilliant one could look at it for only a moment, then blink, turn away, and look again. About it was a sense of antiquity, ancient skills and arts lost and forgotten.

Whether or not it originated with Sheba and Solomon, it was obviously a rarity, a priceless object. Though it stood on an altar, the Llongo did not worship it as an idol. It was a good luck charm, symbol and soul of the people. It was not behind locked bars because the people always wanted it free and open, where they could see it. Though thievery was not unknown in the jungle, it never occurred to anyone that the image might be stolen.

On that day, as they stood before the gleaming image, he asked High Chief Llionto about possible theft. Llionto laughed.

"Would any man, woman or child of Llongo steal his own good luck?"

"Not by a Llongo. By an outsider, Llionto."

Llionto no longer laughed. His face was serious as he spoke. "There is a curse upon it. Only one of Llongo blood may touch it. Let anyone else—and he dies."

The Phantom's silence may have been interpreted as skepticism. High Chief Llionto went on to explain. Originally, the curse had been laid upon the image by that son of Solomon who founded the Llongo people. It is well known that Solomon was familiar with djinns and demons, and the son had learned his father's secrets. Needless to say, the legend was not often challenged. But when it was . . . Llionto recalled an episode of his youth. A thief had come by night, a man of mixed blood (Llionto spat out the phrase showing the Llongo disapproval of intermarriage). This halfbreed had gotten his hands on the image and reached the front gates. There, eyewitnesses swore, the image had twisted and squirmed in his arms, finally stabbing him in the chest with its long sharp horns. He died on the spot

"And this is not gossip," said Llionto. "For that man was known to us, the illegitimate son" (he used a coarse Llongo phrase) "of Onatta of Oogaan and a pale outsider."

No, the sacred image had always been there, and always would be. And was, until now.

The sound of the waterfall was louder now. Both Hero and Devil pricked up their ears and ran faster. They were nearing home, the Deep Woods. The thickets and underbrush were almost impassable here. If you didn't know the hidden twists and turns in the heavy growth, you'd need a tank to get through. Hero and Devil knew the twists and turns. Now a sharp little face appeared among the leaves in a tree above. Another little face rose out of a thicket, then the little shoulders and muscular arms. They held small bows and arrows, and they smiled happily as the great white stallion picked out his way through the dense vegetation.

These were the outer sentries of the Bandar, the pygmy poison people, and the sight of them would send any jungle-man, even the bravest warrior, into headlong flight. For their poisons, bringing instant death, were well known. The Bandar were peaceful little folk who liked the privacy of their shadowy world and resented intrusions.

But this was no stranger. They greeted him happily in their

click-clack tongue, and a young pygmy, Huran, son of their Chief, Guran, dropped from a bough onto Hero's broad back. Only Huran dared such intimacy, since the Phantom was his godfather. Together on Hero, the grinning little youngster and the powerful hooded rider, a giant in comparison, plunged through the roaring waterfall that was the secret entrance to the heart of the Deep Woods, and the fabulous Skull Cave and Skull Throne of the Phantom, the Ghost Who Walks.

He was greeted happily by Rex, his twelve-year-old ward, Rex's buddy Tomm, their tutor Miss Tagama, Chief Guran, Old Man Mozz (the Teller of Tales), and a dozen pygmies. After kisses and hugs for Rex and salutations for the others, he asked about the Llongo theft. They'd heard about it, but the pygmies were not interested. What went on in the outside world among the big people was remote and unimportant. But Rex, Miss Tagama and Old Mozz wanted more details. He told them all he knew about the image, including the death of the would-be thief Llionto had told him about. Miss Tagama frowned at that, but Rex was enchanted.
"Bloody fairy tales," she said.
"All true," said Old Man Mozz, the ancient Teller of Tales, who knew everything and forgot nothing. "More than once it happened in this way, and more than once the image struck down the outsider as the curse of old times foretold. I could tell you many a tale about that sacred image continued the old man in his singsong voice.
"Later, Old Mozz," said the Phantom, for Rex, grinning wickedly at Tomm, had just handed him a small blue envelope.
"It's from Diana. I could tell from the perfume," he shouted happily to Tomm. "It came tonight by monkey mail."
The Phantom chuckled, patted Rex on the head and walked casually into the Skull Cave. As soon as he was out of their sight, he rushed to the closest burning wall torch. As he opened the envelope and took out the note, he thought of the voyage this small letter had had—from Diana's desk by her garden window, to a mailbox, a plane overseas; picked up at Mawitaan's general post office, Box 7, Mr. Walker (for the Ghost Who Walks); taken by the boy, Tona, to the jungle's edge where the regular jungle delivery took off fleet relay runners, clad only in loincloth and mailbag; on to the edge of the Great Swamp and the cages of chimps, where the old man put the letter in a leather pouch tied to a chimp's back; the chimp swinging through the trees over the Great Swamp to his perch and the reward of a banana near the Skull Throne. Shorter messages—cables and the like—came by air, tied to the leg of Fraka, the Phantom's fierce falcon.

"Darling," the letter began in Diana's fine script. The Phantom read on:

Will this come to you by monkey mail? How marvelous! I only wish I could be there to see it arrive out of the trees on the back of one of those dear chimps. I am well—lonely without you. How long has it been? Ages.

I'm going to Paris next month with my UN medical team for one of those conferences. (The kind that go on and on.) If you would just happen to be on that part of the planet at the same time, wouldn't it be wonderful? Just a long shot, but I thought I'd mention it.

All my love,
Diana

"All my love." The words seemed to burn off the page. Wouldn't it be wonderful? Yes, wonderful, fabulous, Diana, he said half aloud, visualizing her cloud of black hair, her large gray eyes, her perfect lips. Ah, Diana. Yes, it has been ages.

Once again, the old conflict. Could he ask this girl to live in a cave, surrounded by pygmies, as his mother and all the wives of the Phantom had done before her? Diana— raised to wealth and comfort, loving theater, opera, ballet. Diana—Olympic gold medalist (high dive), now a vital cog in the United Nations medical program. He had often thought about this. So, he knew, had she. So far, no answers.

He noted the dates, the place where she'd be staying. Who knows? he told himself. Her letter could be an omen that something just might happen to take him to "that part of the planet."

He was busied with numerous details during the next few weeks. On his return, he had immediately contacted the Jungle Patrol headquarters in Mawitaan. Using his radio transmitter in the Skull Cave, he sent word to Colonel Worobu, black commanding officer of the Patrol, to query the *Moru Benga* concerning Old Murph. Word came back a week later. The captain of the *Moru Benga*, reached at the port of Ivory-Lana up the coast, knew nothing. The deceased had not been a passenger aboard the ship, and was unknown to him. That seemed to end that.

Further queries made by the Patrol in and about Mawitaan gave no clue to Old Murph's death. He hadn't been seen in his usual hangouts for some time, had no known enemies. Everybody liked Old Murph. He was known to be fond of the bottle. The consensus was that he had gotten drunk in one of those waterfront saloons and had toppled off a pier. When the wharf crowd heard he was gone, nobody was surprised. Old Murph had one too many and had stumbled once too often. That was his epitaph.

This exchange of information, Skull Cave to Jungle Patrol Headquarters, took place over what was known to patrolmen as the X Band. This was the private frequency of the Commander of the Jungle Patrol, who stood at the top of the chain of command (Colonel Worobu was just below); whose private office, containing only a bare safe, was always locked, and who remained anonymous and unknown. This fact always puzzled Patrol recruits. After a year or two of asking questions, and receiving no answers, they would give up.

The mystery of Old Murph and his dying words were filed somewhere in the Phantom's memory bank, not to be forgotten. And the theft of the Llongo sacred image faded from his mind for the time being, engrossed as he was in a dozen odds and ends—rescuing a missionary from bandits, finding a lost Wambesi child, destroying a killer leopard, and so on. During all this, Diana's letter remained fresh in his mind. Wouldn't it be wonderful? Would they meet on that part of the planet? Was the letter an omen? As it turned out, it was. But he wouldn't know that until later. Like most omens, it would be revealed by hindsight.

He began to consider a return to Eden, when Fraka, the falcon, whizzed down from the sky like a rocket. In the cylinder attached to his leg was a brief message:

"I need your help. Please visit my people. Luaga."

CHAPTER 3

Dr. Lamanda Luaga, Llongo-born Rhodes Scholar, 10th Degree Judo-Karate black belt, Olympic light-heavyweight champion, had served with Diana Palmer on a United Nations medical team in the Bangalla jungle. During the civil war, he fought against the insurgent General Bababu, and was elected first President of the new nation of Bangalla. The Phantom had aided him in some of this, and they were fast friends. A request from him was serious and urgent. The Phantom wasted no time. Within minutes of having taken the message from Fraka, he saddled Hero and raced through the waterfall with Devil close to Hero's flying heels.

"What was that all about?" asked Miss Tagama.

"He didn't say," said Rex.

With the Phantom, to think was to act. When he vanished through that waterfall, they never knew if he was going for; a dip in a nearby pool, or leaving the continent—to be gone an hour or a month.

He rode for a day and a night, making only brief stops to rest, water and feed his animals and himself. Hero grazed on the rich grass along the streams where they camped. Devil ranged for meat, returning with hare, one for himself, one for his master. The long gray wolf preferred his meat uncooked. The Phantom liked his medium-rare. After a meal and an hour of sleep, they would be off again, the hoofs of the great white stallion thundering through the quiet woods.

Small animals scurried out of sight. Monkeys chattered in the trees, birds scattered. A leopard watched them from a high bough, but decided against a leap. The man, horse and wolf looked too formidable. And so they were. With Hero's sharp hoofs, Devil's long fangs and the Phantom's firepower, they were a match for anything that moved in the jungle. In this fashion, racing, resting briefly, moving again, they reached the Llongo gates. It was immediately apparent to him that there had been a change.

Part of the wall was smashed by a huge tree that had fallen on it, evidently the result of a recent storm. Inside the walls, several huts had been demolished, perhaps by the same storm. How long had it been since he visited here? About five months. How long since the image had vanished? About half that time. As he rode through the gates, one of which hung loosely on a broken hinge, he glanced at the covered altar where he had last seen the image. It was empty. No guard in sight. A crowd gathered quickly around him, but it wasn't the same happy laughing crowd he remembered from that last visit. They were quiet. They looked despondent. They seemed frightened. He walked on to the big hut of Llionto. The High Chief was seated on a pile of straw. As the Phantom approached, two warriors helped the old man to his feet. He stood with some difficulty, leaning on a cane.

"I had a small accident," he explained as the Phantom looked at him questioningly. "A leg of my throne broke. I fell—almost broke my back."

There was quiet sobbing from a corner. The beautiful eighteen-year-old bride sat there, almost unrecognizable, her face swollen out of shape.

"Stung by a swarm of bees," said Llionto.

"Please, don't stand on my account," said the Phantom anxiously.

"Now that I'm up, it's easier than sitting. Oh, Phantom friend, since we lost our sacred image, it's been awful. Everything has gone wrong."

"Llionto, a swarm of bees, a breaking chair—those things can happen to anyone," said the Phantom.

"You saw the tree that destroyed part of our wall? Last week. A terrible storm. It demolished three huts as well. Then, the next night, a tiger got into our goat pens. It was terrible."

"Llionto, you are a wise and rational man. You must know these things are a coincidence."

"Coincidence?" snorted the High Chief. "We are no longer winning at the track. Not one winner in three weeks. Whilst in Mawitaan, my own son Lomo got into the usual poker game at the Blue Dragon, lost every cent he had, plus IOU's. Even that money was borrowed, for he had been robbed by bandits on the way to Mawitaan."

"Llionto," said the Phantom weakly, only half believing his

own words, "these things can happen to anybody and often do."

"But not to Llongo!" roared the old High Chief. "Before our sacred image was stolen, Lomo never lost in the poker game at the Blue Dragon. He was never attacked by bandits. Our people always won at the track. Tigers never got into our goat pens. Storms never damaged our village. Bees never stung our women. And my throne never broke."

Exhausted and shaken by all this bad luck, the huge old man signaled the waiting warriors who carefully lowered him down to the piles of straw.

"Tell me about the theft of the image. Do you know who did it?"

"We know."

"But you've told me it is protected by the curse. No outsider may touch it and live."

"True."

"That means . . . ?"

"That means, I am ashamed to say, a man of Llongo did it. My own no-good nephew Loka."

"How do you know that?"

The old chief pointed to the side. There was a wooden cage there, with heavy ironwood bars, the sort used to hold big cats. A young Llongo warrior sat inside the cage, head lowered, his face in his hands. Llionto told what had happened.

Loka, the ne'er-do-well, had come by night while the rest of the village slept. The man in the cage had been on guard duty that night. Loka offered him a bottle of beer, which he accepted. It is against the rules to drink while on duty, but Loka had persuaded the young guard. What harm in a bottle of beer? In the morning, the guard was found by the altar in a drunken sleep, a beer bottle at his side. The sacred image was gone.

"That's how it happened," said Llionto bitterly.

"What will you do to him?"

"Thanks to you, my father banned the old punishment, death by beheading," said Llionto. The Phantom reflected. His father or, perhaps, his grandfather Phantom had done that. "Otherwise, the fool would lose his head," said Llionto. "Now, I don't know. We are so mixed up."

"Did Loka live in the village?"

"Him? No, he left years ago for the life in town. We hardly ever saw him here. He'd taken up with a putzka" —the Llongo word for a non-Llongo of alien race, white or Asian—"and was always in trouble. A bad sort."

"I'll ask you more about Loka in a moment. What have you done so far to recover the image?"

"Done? Sent out word to all the jungle. Sent my own son, Loma, to report the disaster to our own Lamanda in Mawitaan."

Lamanda was President Luaga, who'd sent the call for help on the leg of Fraka, the falcon.

"Loma, tell him what happened."

Loma, son of the chief, stepped out of the shadows of the hut. He was a husky young man, handsome like all Llongo males. His arm was in a sling; his head was bandaged.

"How did you hurt your arm, Loma?"

"I fell out of a tree," said the young man, embarrassed,

"Never before, in his entire life, has he fallen out of a tree," said High Chief Llionto.

"And your head?"

"Bandits, on the way to Mawitaan to see my cousin Lamanda."

Loma told his story. When the theft was discovered, his father sent him at once to the capital to report to Lamanda Luaga. The President was Llongo, the smartest of all of them, and he would know what to do. On the way, Loma reported the following incidents: he fell into a tiger trap, stepped on a porcupine and was hit with a score of painful quills, almost drowned and was bitten by fish in crossing a stream, and finally was attacked by bandits who took all his money and beat him.

"In all the history of our people, no Llongo has ever suffered such disasters," shouted Llionto.

Loma continued. When he reached the city and the palace gates where his cousin lived, the guards refused him entrance. "And no wonder," he explained. "I was bruised and bleeding and muddy and filthy. I pleaded and begged, while they laughed when I said Lamanda was my cousin. Though I was weak and hungry and tired, that angered me. I said that I was Llongo, and Llongo people did not lie. This, they knew, as all jungle people know. And one who was kinder than the others talked into a telephone, and soon I was taken into the palace, the home of Lamanda."

His eyes widened and all the people in the hut listened enthralled as he described the magnificence of the presidential palace—the marble staircase, the rich hangings, the blazing chandeliers, the polished floors. Lamanda remembered him, greeted him warmly ("hugged me," Loma assured his listeners, who had all heard this tale before but were eager to hear it again). He called in his own physician to dress Loma's wounds. He was given a bath in an enormous bathroom and fed a, wonderful dinner. Lamanda asked him endless questions about the village and relatives and old friends. Then ha told Lamanda what had happened. He told him all he knew.

The news seemed to stun Lamanda. He sat at his desk in deep thought for many minutes. Loma noticed a small replica of the sacred image on his desk. (The others nodded. Lamanda had not forgotten his people.) Then Lamanda said he would do what he could. He also offered Loma a job if he wished to remain in the city. But Loma refused. He wished to return to the village. But first, a game at the Blue

Dragon. Lamanda lent him the money for the game, since the bandits had stripped him clean. The poker players finished the job, and Loma returned to his home.

That's how Lamanda Luaga had learned of the theft. He must have sent the message to the Deep Woods right after that. The Phantom could visualize him riding in his long official limousine, flags flying, motorcycle escorts fore and aft, roaring up to the little hut at the jungle's edge where Toma's father kept the homing pigeon cotes and the cage of Fraka.

Llionto and the others in the big hut were smiling happily during Loma's tale of his visit to the presidential palace, enjoying the reflected glory of their own Lamanda Luaga who had made it so big. Now, as the Phantom continued questioning, they became glum again. Back to unlucky reality.

"Could I talk to the guard . . . the prisoner?"

Llionto nodded. He was lifted to his feet again, and the whole crowd followed to the wooden cage. The young man inside looked at the Phantom fearfully. Was his crime so enormous that the Phantom himself had come? In answering the Phantom's questions, his story was the same as the High Chief's. The beer bottle itself, prime evidence, was tied to a bar.

"How many beers did you drink?"

"One, I think."

"Could one bottle make you drunk?"

The man behind the bars looked confused. It didn't seem possible, yet . . . The Phantom sniffed the bottle, then called the High Chief.

"Smell this." The Chief did. "Is that the way your beer smells?"

"Not exactly."

"It was drugged." The Phantom explained. The smell was that of a powerful sleeping powder not known in the jungle. "Your nephew Loka"—the Chief shuddered at that— "drugged the guard. This man is not to blame."

That was a vast relief to the man in the cage and to his family and friends who had gathered to listen. But it did not change anything.

"When did you last see Loka, before that night?"

He had visited the village a week before, with his putzka and a white man. They'd all come in Old Murph's car.

"Old Murph?" The Phantom's mind reeled for a moment, memory banks clicking. "Are you certain it was Old Murph?"

"Of course. We spoke. We were old friends. He often came here with visitors, tourists. We heard he died. Drowned. More bad luck," said Llionto sadly.

Memory banks purring, sights and sounds coming back.

"Llionto, you told me, when you were a young man, you saw an outsider try to steal the sacred image. It killed him. True?"

"True."

"Did you see the wounds made by the sacred image?"

"I did."

"Do you remember what these wounds looked like?"

"Who could forget? The wounds were made by the horns of the sacred image. Sharp points, like two thin daggers. Two wounds at the heart. Small, round, deep."

Small, round, deep. At the heart, like Old Murph's wounds.

The dying whisper came back. "Damn thing . . . damn thing . . . true . . . true . . . how you like that . . . "

CHAPTER 4

There are times, it is said, when the Phantom leaves the jungle and comes to the town as an ordinary man. This was one of those times.

At a hidden corral near the jungle's edge, he left Hero, the white stallion, with young Tona. Here, the Phantom changed his outer garb, putting on trousers, a topcoat, hat, sunglasses and a scarf that concealed the costume underneath. Then, with Devil at his side, he strode into the town, out of the foggy night.

As he walked through the dimly lit, quiet and deserted streets—it was late and most of the honest citizens of this tropical capital were asleep—he turned the events over in his mind. The linking of Old Murph to the theft of the sacred image ... no, not really. No one said the old man had been there that night, although someone had heard a car drive off. Old Murph's ancient Landrover? And those wounds—like the puncture of an ice pick. No answers yet. Maybe Lamanda Luaga had some.

When he reached the palace gates, it was about three o'clock in the morning. A high picket fence surrounded the extensive lawns and gardens. Before the revolution, led by Lamanda, this had been the colonial governor's mansion. The Phantom approached the two sleepy guards at the closed gates. They snapped to alertly, rifles in hands, looking suspiciously at this tall stranger wearing dark sunglasses in the middle of the night. And the long gray animal—a dog? No dog they'd ever seen had pale blue eyes like these, eyes that gleamed in the feeble light. No dog they knew had fangs that big. The stranger asked to see the President. Important, he said. They couldn't help laughing.

"See the President at this hour. Are you crazy?"

"Got an appointment?" asked the other one, bringing up his rifle.

"No appointment. But he'll see me."

"And who shall we say is calling?" said the first guard, with mock politeness.

"Mr. Walker."

"*Mister* Walker," said the second guard. "May I inquire as to the nature of your business?"

"You may not," said Mr. Walker calmly.

The two guards level their rifles at him.

"You're under arrest," said the first guard.

"What did I do?"

"Coming here, at this hour? You're either crazy or an assassin."

With that last word, they both stopped smiling and were grim. The dark sunglasses faced them for a moment.

"Assassin?" he said. "How about them?" He looked to the side. They both followed his glance. As they looked away, he snatched their rifles from their hands. As quick as that. Their heads popped back, looking at their empty hands, then at the muzzles of their rifles pointing toward them. ("Phantom moves like lightning in the sky," went an old jungle saying.)

"Turn around," he said in the same calm tone. Bewildered, they obeyed. "Don't move," said the voice. They could imagine those rifles pointed at their heads. They remained as they were for a full minute. No more sounds. They listened as hard as they could for the slightest sound. There was nothing. Not even breathing. One guard turned his head cautiously. The first thing he saw out of the corner of his eye was the two rifles stacked against the gatepost. He and his partner whirled about, grabbing the rifles. They looked into the foggy darkness beyond the gate lights. The man and the animal were nowhere to be seen. Had he gotten onto the palace grounds? They rushed into their booth and phoned an immediate alert to the palace staff. An assassin or madman was in the area, on the loose.

After placing the rifles down, the Phantom and Devil had walked off a few paces, soundlessly. ("The Phantom moves on cat's feet.") At his master's signal, the wolf remained, concealing himself in a clump of bushes next to the curb. The Phantom vaulted lightly over the picket fence and moved quickly across the dark lawn—all this before the guards turned around.

There was a knock on the President's office door. This was a large suite, part office, part bedroom. Lamanda Luaga, first President of Bangalla, stirred under the covers as the knocking persisted, then snapped on his bedside light.

"Yes?" he called, irritated and sleepy. It had been a hard day.

The office door opened. An officer peered in.

"Some trouble at the front gate. Just wanted to make sure you are all right, sir."

"What trouble?"

"A man trying to see you."

Lamanda glanced at his bedside clock.

"At this hour?"

"Obviously crazy, sir, or . . ." The officer cleared his throat.

"An assassin?" said Lamanda, sitting up. "Assassins do not announce themselves at the front gate, at this hour. Did they get him?"

"Seems he managed to escape, sir."

"Anything else?"

"Said his name was Walker."

Lamanda Luaga smiled "That will be all, Colonel."

"Sir, we'll post guards around your suite, just in case."

"That won't be necessary, Colonel. Good night."

The door closed. Lamanda got out of bed, and had just finished tying the belt of his dressing gown when the French doors leading to the garden opened and the Phantom stepped in. The two men shook hands warmly, old friends meeting.

"I should have known it was you at once," said Luaga. "Who else would upset my guards at this hour. How did you get in?"

"Over the fence."

"Those guards have rifles."

"Had."

Luaga grinned. "They're good boys. I hope you didn't hurt them."

"No violence."

The Phantom removed his outer garments, and was once more the hooded, masked figure. Luaga heated up coffee on an electric burner on a sideboard, and the two settled at the wide desk for a talk. The Phantom noticed the little replica of the sacred image.

"You know all about that," he said.

"Only that it was stolen."

"You know what it means to your people."

"I know. I know what it means to me. I am here, in this

palace," said the famed scholar-athlete-leader. "Take the boy out of the jungle; can't take the jungle out of the boy," he added with a short laugh.

"Have you found out anything more?"

"My intelligence people looked into it, didn't find much. The image may still be in the country, though I doubt it."

"You know who was involved?"

"One evidently was a white man, known as Duke. Background as a mercenary, soldier of fortune, smuggler, barroom brawler. The other one"—he hesitated—"was a Llongo."

—"His name is Loka. A nephew of the Chief."

Lamanda Luaga, President of Bangalla, sighed, and glanced over the top of his coffee cup at his masked visitor.

"I know," he said. "He's my brother."

For a moment, the room was heavy with silence.

"That's a surprise."

"Yes, isn't it. We're both nephews of Llionto." He picked up the little replica of the sacred image, the two-headed bull, and turned it over and over as he spoke of his brother.

"This sacred image, the luck of the Llongo, didn't do him much good," he began. "He was four years older, always wild and undisciplined, even as a kid. Used to bully me when we were small. He was bigger and heavier. Maybe I developed faster, in self-defense. I learned karate from an Asian kid in the missionary school. By the time I was twelve, I could take Loka. After that, he let me alone."

Lamanda Luaga chuckled. "Odd how things turn out. I'd probably never have gotten that athletic scholarship and wound up winning the Olympic gold medal if it hadn't been for those early beatings my brother gave me. I worked hard. While I won scholarships, academic as well as athletic, Loka cheated in school and was thrown out. He continued to cheat at everything after that. Tampering with cards and dice, doping horses at the track, that sort of thing. Meantime, I'd left Bangalla and gone to England for premed and medical school. The Rhodes scholarship did that for me. I continually received cables from Loka for money. When I returned, a doctor, I got him out of a dozen scrapes. His friends were the riffraff—cheap gamblers, thieves, smugglers —the underworld of this seaport town. As a doctor, my pay was small. He kept me broke. I finally told him to leave me alone. It was a bad scene. We stopped seeing each other. That was long before I got into politics."

By this time, Lamanda was pacing the floor, still holding the little image.

"But this," he said, his voice rising angrily as he held up the image, "this is the worst thing he could do to our people. He has disgraced our family."

His voice broke and he breathed deeply to control himself. The Llongo are emotional people.

"Lamanda, why would he do it?"

"Can't you guess?"

"Money, I suppose. It must have some value."

"Some value? What would you guess? You've seen it."

"I haven't the slightest idea."

Lamanda opened a drawer and took out two newspapers. One was a Paris daily newspaper. The other was a London Sunday supplement. Both papers featured a large photo of the two-headed bull, and a long story about its history. Also, it's estimated value. The Phantom whistled.

"Can that be true? I didn't know the image was so well known."

"It wasn't known, until about two years ago," explained Luaga. "Two art dealers from London heard about it while on a tour here. They came to me to ask if it were permissible by our laws to purchase such antiques and take them out of the country. I told them that none of the art treasures of our country were for sale. They belonged to the nation. As for the sacred image of the Llongo, that was the most treasured and could never leave its village. One of them laughed—I recall his name was Helmsley. He said everything has a price and mentioned one for the image. It bowled me over."

"How much?"

"One million English pounds. At the current rate, about two and a half million dollars."

"This article says two million English pounds," said the Phantom, reading the newspaper.

"Prices have gone up."

"But how could they put a price on it, without seeing it?"

"Oh, but they did see it. They drove out to the village and examined it closely—without touching, of course. One even had a jeweler's eyeglass. You see, it's not just the value of the thing itself. It's the age. The experts say it is pre-Christian era, perhaps four thousand years old, a completely unique piece."

The Phantom's memory banks were clicking again, new data registering, surfacing, forming.

"There are no regular roads to the Llongo village. Two strangers, English tourists, would have a hard time driving there alone."

Lamanda Luaga looked slightly annoyed at this digression. "Obviously they had a guide."

"Do you recall who the guide was?"

The President looked at him, perplexed. But he concentrated. The Phantom never wasted words, or questions.

"Yes, I do remember. In fact, they'd asked me about a guide. I only knew one who was honest, who knew the jungle, and would be well received by my people. Poor old chap died recently."

"Old Murph?"

"Yes. How did you know? I remember telling them there was no point in making the long trip, since the image was not for sale. They said they were art lovers and only wanted to see it."

"Lamanda, Old Murph didn't just die. He was murdered. It now seems obvious that his death was involved with the missing image."

"Murder?"

The Phantom nodded and told him the story of finding the old man offshore of Eden, the wounds, the dying words, the burial at sea. "It's a bit clearer now, but not completely so. Old Murph guides those English art dealers to the village. On the return he hears them discussing it, evaluating it. Perhaps later, in some bar, he talks. Maybe no one takes him seriously at first. A million English pounds for an old jungle idol! Then somebody takes him seriously. Another tour to the Llongo village—your brother Loka, his putzka"—the President laughed at that—"and a big white man, possibly the one called Duke."

"It begins to make sense," said Luaga. "The bar could have been the Blue Dragon, Loka's hangout."

"They heard a car drive off the night of the theft. Old Murph's."

Both men sat quietly for a moment. Luaga sighed deeply.

"You've helped me before. I need you now more than ever. This is a scandal that could rock my administration. The country's greatest art treasure, stolen by my brother. The murder of Old Murph."

"But you've had no part in any of this," said the Phantom.

"We put down the counter revolt by the army; you remember General Bababu. We established this democracy. But the old officer clique is still around, waiting for me to slip, waiting for a chance to smash our young legislature, our courts, our democracy, and take over with an iron hand. We have military dictatorships on both borders ready to, help them, to move in. They hate our democracy. It might give their own people ideas."

It was like sitting in a small room and suddenly seeing the roof and walls open up to a vast panorama.

"Is it that serious?" said the Phantom, knowing it was.

"You know this country as well as I do. Do you think I

exaggerate?"

"No," said the Phantom. "It could happen. We must not let it happen."

"As soon as I received this news, my special unit checked out the airport, wharfs, bars, all Loka's known crowd. The one called Duke had disappeared. Loka's girl, a Eurasian dancer at the Blue Dragon, was no help. We didn't know she had been with Loka on that visit to the image. Understand, I couldn't have too wide an investigation. That might expose everything, before we could solve it."

The Phantom got up and put on his street clothes—trousers, coat, hat, sunglasses and scarf.

"You can't touch this, Lamanda. You're too vulnerable. This new country you put together is too fragile. Your fears for it are well founded. If you go out of power now, the nation might not survive. That means civil war, terror, all over again."

"Fantastic, that this little incident could be the cause," said Luaga, fingering the image.

"I must move fast now. If you are questioned about any of this, you know nothing."

Lamanda nodded. "What now?"

"I've a few leads. What is the name of that girl, Loka's friend?"

Lamanda riffled through his desk and found a small notebook.

"Sala. At the Blue Dragon."

CHAPTER 5

The Blue Dragon was the biggest, toughest, noisiest saloon in Mawitaan. It boasted the longest bar, the hottest gambling, and the best floor show on the coast. The last item was nothing much to write home about. The so-called floor show was only a showcase for most of the aging "girls" who conducted their serious profession in rooms upstairs, but not for the star, Sala. Sala was something else, the Phantom decided as he stood watching at the crowded bar. She was doing her own version of an Oriental belly dance, and was driving the rough crowd—nine-tenths sailors and longshoremen—wild. Lean and exotic, she was as sinuous as a cobra, with a suggestion of that reptile's danger in her flashing eyes and cruel smile.

He was jammed in among the boisterous gang at the bar. Devil, on a leash, sat at his feet. A bartender finally reached him.

"What'll it be?"

"Glass of milk. A saucer of water for my animal, please."

"Milk?" shouted the bartender. The men near the Phantom quieted and turned to look at him, this tall stranger in the dark wraparound sunglasses. "Are you kidding?"

"No, I want a glass of milk . . . and water for my animal," said the Phantom quietly. He hadn't wanted to attract this attention. He was thirsty, and since he never drank alcoholic beverages, and was unfamiliar, with soft drinks, milk was all he could think of.

This bartender, and a half dozen others working behind the bar, were used to all sorts in this place. Wise guys, tough guys, drunks, crazies. It was a busy place, and they wasted no time with nuisances. They were used to sizing up such types quickly. This one, the bartender quickly decided, was a wise guy.

"This is no dairy farm," he said loudly, for the benefit of the appreciative audience on the other side of the bar. "And we got no time for flea hounds. Get lost, stupid."

The listeners laughed at this, and others crowded around to hear the fun. This particular bartender's blistering wit was well known.

The Phantom was not looking for a fight. He was here on business, and would have preferred to slip out of this argument quietly. The word "stupid" stung, but he held his temper.

"You have a public license. If I order a reasonable drink of milk, you are obliged to serve it," he said quietly. "Asking water for my dog is also a reasonable request."

The bartender was exasperated. A half-dozen customers were yelling orders, and this wise guy was going on and on.

"Listen, you want me to call the bouncer," he shouted.

"You—!" That was a mistake. The epithet he used could not be ignored. In one quick move, the Phantom grasped the two-hundred-pounder by the neck, dragged him bodily across the bar, then lifted him over his head and hurled him into the air. The big man flew ten feet, and landed with a crash on the dance floor where Sala was in the midst of her sexy gyrations. She froze, uttered a slight yelp, and ran off the floor. The crowd at the bar cheered and laughed, particularly one man standing near the Phantom. He was a head taller than the others, had a full dark beard, and wore a blue cap and pea jacket—a seaman. His laughter was a deep rumble and his heavy accent could be heard above the others.

"Goot, goot," he said.

Two heavyset husky men in T-shirts moved rapidly to the bar. They were the Blue Dragon bouncers, veterans of trouble.

"What's your trouble?" one of them said belligerently as he reached out to grab the Phantom's arm.

"I gave him an order. He refused and swore at me. I don't accept that kind of language."

"Aren't you the sweet fella," said the bouncer, tightening his grip. "You want to get your tail outta here before you get hurt?"

"No, I don't," said the Phantom.

"Yeah?" said the bouncer. He pulled the arm, to drag the man out. But nothing happened. It was like pulling on the branch of a tree. The Phantom didn't stir. The bouncer's expression of amazement was ludicrous. His face turned red.

"You get outta here, or we'll throw you out on your keister," he shouted, angered by the snickers of the watching crowd. Another man in the Phantom's position might have decided that retreat was the smartest move, considering the mission. But the Phantom wasn't another man. He had a stubborn streak that resented injustice of any kind, and he felt this treatment was unjust. He was the innocent party. And when the second bouncer reached for him, he knew the time for action had come again. He lashed out twice with his iron fists – not hard enough to kill (which he could do), but hard enough to end the problem of these bouncers. The two blows, one on each jaw, did the job. The two big men hit the floor solidly, bounced, then lay still. There were gasps from those nearby. Nobody had ever taken one of these bouncers, much less two. The big saloon was quiet for a moment. People at tables turned toward the bar. Even the distant players at the card and dice tables peered through the smoke to see what had happened. Then the big bearded seaman added his deep rumbling laughter. "Goot job, man," he said, and reached over to pound the Phantom on the back.

A small fat Oriental in a white suit, sweat on his bald head and a glittering diamond stickpin in his tie, rushed up. "Whasa matta, whasa matta here?" he asked excitedly.

"I asked for milk and water for my dog. The bartender refused. Your bouncers tried to throw me out," said the Phantom patiently.

"And a goot job he did," boomed the bearded seaman.

"For goonasake, give man milk, give dog wata, start music," the Oriental shouted shrilly. He was the proprietor of the Blue Dragon, and this pause in the drinking was costing him money. The three-piece band started up again, the people at the bar laughed, and the card and dice players went back to the games. Six waiters, staggering under the weight of the bartender and the bouncers, cleared the dance floor. The crowd cheered, couples began to dance, drink were served, the dice clicked, and the fight was forgotten. Such fracases were a nightly happening at the Blue Dragon. The only difference was that this time the bouncers were on the receiving end. As for the Phantom, he got his glass of milk, Devil got his saucer of water, and after a few slaps on the back and offers of drinks by the bearded seaman, which were politely refused, the gang at the bar went back to their glasses. The big guy in the sunglasses was obviously a tough customer, but such types were not rare in the Blue Dragon.

The Phantom was annoyed with himself. He had come

here to talk to Sala and learn what he could about Loka. The fracas could have spoiled everything. He promised himself to hold his temper and turn the other cheek in the future, or at least until this baffling situation was solved. Sala had not returned.

He moved slowly through the crowd, Devil following closely. He walked between the intense, grim players at the card tables (where Loma, son of High Chief Llionto, had played and lost), among the shouting dice players, and went through the beaded curtain where he had seen Sala exit. An angry argument was going on in a room down the hall. It was Sala's dressing room. The Oriental proprietor was trying to get her back on the dance floor. She was refusing. The fight had upset her.

"That guy, flying through the air, he almost hit me. Could have killed me," she shouted.

"Did not kill, did not hurt. All finish. All quiet. You go back now, Sala. Crowd wants."

"Sala doesn't want. Leave me, Wong. I'm finished for tonight."

"Finished for tonight?" screamed Mr. Wong. "You crazy?"

"You heard me. No more tonight. Get lost," she screamed. Then both quieted suddenly as they noticed the tall stranger in the doorway. Both recognized him—the man in sunglasses.

"I want to talk to you, Sala," he said.

"I don't allow men in my dressing room," she said, staring at the dark glasses.

"She gotta dance. She gotta work, mister," said Mr. Wong.

"You heard her. She said she's finished for the night. That's it, Mr. Wong."

Mr. Wong stared up at the big man and licked his lips. People who have heard the deep voice of the Phantom have often tried to describe it. One, a poet, said that "it seemed to come from a deep pit, with all the tremendous authority of the law of gravity." In the jungle it is said, "the voice of the angry Phantom can freeze the tiger's blood." However it was, Mr. Wong heard. Sala also heard it. She clenched her fist as the door closed.

"Leave that open," she said sharply.

"No, Sala. You've nothing to fear from me. I want a private talk with you—about Loka."

That name seemed to jolt her. She sat at her dressing table and waited.

"Where is he?"

She shrugged. "Who knows."

"Do you?"

"No."

"You are his friend?"

"Was."

It went on like that for a while, words-of-one-syllable answers, communicating nothing.

"Sala, about two months or more ago, you took a trip into the jungle with Loka and his friend Duke. You were driven there by Old Murph."

She reacted to that last name. Her long artificial eyelashes waved up and down like wings. She finally put a sentence together.

"Are you a cop?"

"No."

"What?"

"I'm a friend of the Llongo people. They want that image back where it belongs."

"That's all you want?"

"Old Murph was murdered. Did you see it happen?"

She sat quietly for a moment, not answering. He studied her. In repose, she was beautiful, as vividly sensuous as some rare wild orchid. In her turn, she was also studying him, this massive figure that had handled those men out there like bean bags. Sala knew men. But she couldn't see his eyes behind those dark glasses, and his face was like granite. Men usually melted before her, especially when she was in this gauzy belly-dancer outfit that revealed more than it covered. But he seemed unmoved by these highly visible and undeniable charms. Then there was the animal . . . a dog? Bigger than any dog she'd ever seen . . . with pale blue eyes and fangs an inch long. What a pair they were!

"I can't tell you anything about all that," she said finally. "About the thing, or about Old what's-his-name."

"I would guess that you're a liar, Sala," he said quietly.

She thought for a long moment. "There's no point in you calling me names if you expect me to help you," she said, and smiled a warm, alluring smile. Part of it was genuine. Sala had always been attracted by men of strength. This one radiated power.

"Do you want to help me?"

"Perhaps. Girls like myself have to do the best they can. If I help, what's in it for me?" she said brightly, becoming chatty.

"It might keep you out of prison."

"Are you kidding? I haven't done anything wrong," she shouted, surprised by his answer.

"You'll have your day in court to prove that."

"You said you weren't a cop."

"Correct."

"You talk like one."

He walked toward her, then stood over her. He loomed above her like a mountain peak. His deep voice seemed to come from a vast distance.

"Sala, a terrible crime has been committed, worse than you can realize. It may have disastrous consequences. If you help me now, things will be easier for you later on."

"I've done nothing wrong."

"You said that before."

A long silence while Sala meditated. There was no melting, no softness in this man. Like talking to a stone wall.

"I have done nothing wrong," she repeated, and as he clenched a big fist in exasperation, she held up her slim hand. "But I know a man who may be able to help."

"Who?"

"Let him tell you who. If if arrange a meeting, isn't that enough."

"It may be."

"I will go and arrange it. Promise to wait here ... or in the bar ... for one hour. Until I return. If you try to follow me now, I will know. I will not arrange it."

"Should I trust you to come back?"

"Can you?"

"For your own sake, Sala, I hope you do not deceive me. You understand ... for your own sake?"

Once more the deep voice rumbled, like distant storm clouds. She shivered.

"I will come back, honest."

She threw a cloak over her shoulders and darted out. The bells on her ankles, part of her costume, tinkled as she ran down the hall. Wherever she is going, whatever she has in mind, at least the first step has been taken, he told himself. The dressing room air was stuffy, heavy with cheap perfume, powder, stale tobacco smoke. He told Devil to stay in the hall and strolled back through the beaded curtains to watch some of the action, the frantic dice players, the grim poker players. And he waited for Sala.

She was almost as good as her word. An hour and a half later, she waved to him impatiently from the beaded curtain. He was standing among the crowd at the dice table, watching a young black make seven points in a row, doubling his bet each time, letting it pile up, and losing it all on the eighth roll, then shrug and grin and move off to the bar.

The Phantom followed Sala into the back hall where Devil sat waiting. Her head was wrapped in a shawl and she was wet. There was a light warm rain falling as they went through the dark alley and headed for the docks. She hadn't spoken.

"You made the arrangement?" he asked.

She nodded and kept walking as fast as she could. They

were on a wharf now where several coastal freighters were tied up. Each had swaying lights high on the masts, but there were no men on the dark dock. Probably all were at the Blue Dragon. Its tinny music, laughter, and shouts could be heard from here. Sala pointed to a gangplank that led up onto a deck. He glanced along the ship's side to the bow. In the semidarkness, he made out the name lettered there: *Moru Benga.*

Sala started to dart off. He grasped her wrist. She looked at him with large frightened eyes, her face wet in the rain, mascara smudged, makeup running.

"Up there. Waiting. The arrangement," she said.

He started for the gangplank, pulling her along. She resisted.

"No, that wasn't it. You promised," she began.

"I promised nothing. Let's see what kind of arrangement this is."

The deck was empty. The ship swayed slowly with the harbor swell. The wooden sides creaked, the wharf creaked, a ship at night. No lights from the cabins or the bridge.

"Where?" he asked softly, still holding her wrist.

She pointed to the first cabin. He approached it slowly and opened the door. Pitch black inside. His hand had loosened the grip on her wrist; he didn't want to hurt her. Suddenly she jerked free and darted away. As he turned to reach for her, something hit him hard on the back of the head. He blacked out.

CHAPTER 6

The three looked at the figure sprawled on the deck. The short heavy man snapped on a flashlight beam.

"Still got his hat and sunglasses on," he said in a squeaky voice.

"Is he dead?" asked Sala.

"Ten pounds to five he is," said the little man.

"I'll take that bet," said the tall man in his deep rumbling voice. "Turn off that light!" The light went off.

"I hope he is," said Sala.

"Bloodthirsty little witch, aren't you," said the big man. "Let's get him off the deck."

He lifted the Phantom by the shoulders and dragged him toward a cabin door. The small man tried to pick up the legs.

"Wow, weighs a ton," said the big man. "Solid iron."

"See him take those guys in the Blue Dragon?" said the squeaky voice, breathing hard under the load.

"Did I?" said Sala. "I was right in the middle of it."

The voices came through to the Phantom as he was being carried. He kept his eyes closed. His head was racked with pain. They placed him on a bunk. He heard the sound of a match struck, the sound of a glass chimney raised and lowered, a kerosene lamp being lit. A hand at his wrist, pressure against his chest—someone's head?

"I win the ten," said the deep rumbling voice. "He's alive."

He'd heard that voice somewhere before, recently. At the bar. The big bearded seaman. His eyes remained closed, his head throbbing.

"You sure?" The voice of Sala, the exotic dancer.

"Sure as I stand here," began the deep voice. Then: "Sala!" The sound of brief scuffling and struggle, hard breathing.

"You crazy witch," roared the deep voice. "Give me that knife!"

"He's after Loka. He'll get us all hung," shouted the girl hysterically.

"Sit down there and shut up," said the deep voice angrily. Sound of girl sitting. Sound of girl crying, not little-girl crying, but the racking sobs of a desperate woman.

"And knock that off," said the deep voice coldly. "Somebody'll hear you on the wharf." The sobbing stopped, reducing to sniffles.

The Phantom opened his eyes. The two men, standing near him, outlined in the pale light of the kerosene lamp. The big one was the bearded seaman. The other one was short and squat, with the wizened face of a monkey. He held a pistol in one hand, a flashlight in the other. Sala sat on a chest at the side, staring at him, still dressed as she was when he followed her onto the ship. How long ago had that been? In the weak light, she glistened, still wet. Not too long, he decided.

"See? Alive," said the big man. "Hand over the tenner." Monkey-Face snapped on the flashlight. The beam was blinding. The Phantom closed his eyes.

"Off with that damn light," roared the big man. The bright beam snapped off.

"Just wanted to make, sure," he squeaked. The Phantom moved one hand slowly toward his head, to feel where he had been hit. The hand was roughly grabbed.

"Give me that rope," the big seaman snapped, and in a moment he was tying the Phantom's wrists together.

"I seen you in the Blue Dragon, bucko. Taking no chances," he said, laughing as he tightened the rope. His laughter was a deep rumble.

"Wanted to feel my head," said the Phantom weakly.

"See, he talks."

"Worse luck," snapped Sala.

"What did you hit me with?"

"This," said the seaman, holding up a short club.

"Quite a sock," said the Phantom.

"Not the first time I've used it, or the last. I wasn't about to kill you, bucko, till I found out what you're about."

The Phantom remained quiet for a moment, concentrating

on the back of his head. He felt no break of any great size. He could only hope there was no fracture or concussion. The scarf, wrapped around his neck, had absorbed part of the blow. And at the moment of impact, reaching out for Sala, he had been moving away from the blow. That may have saved him from serious injury. Without showing any outward movement, he flexed his muscles slightly, from jaw to toes. Everything checked out. All systems go, he told himself. Except for the aching head. He was astonished to realize that his two guns were still snug in their holsters beneath the outer clothing. Either it hadn't occurred to his captors to frisk him, or they hadn't gotten to that yet.

"Who are you?" he said weakly. Though his strength was surging back, he would maintain the beaten, exhausted pretense.

"I don't mind answering that," began the seaman.

"None of his damn business," snapped Sala. "Ask him who he is."

"Woman, would you shut that sweet little mouth before I give you a good one across the chops," said the seaman angrily. She quieted immediately. Obviously, he had given her "one across the chops" in the past.

"Everyone knows me," said the big seaman, his accent heavier now—Germanic or Scandinavian. "I am Sven Ohlsson, owner unt captain of the *Moru Benga*."

"Is this the way you usually treat visitors on your ship. Captain?" said the Phantom.

"Visitor? You are a trespasser, a prowler. Who could criticize if I shot you? I vould be vithin my rights."

"I came here at the invitation of Sala to meet someone."

Captain Sven Ohlsson laughed heartily at that, as if it was a big joke. Little Monkey-Face contributed a cackle.

"She is not goot vitness for you. She tried to stab you," he went on, slapping his leg. "All right. Who are you? What do you vant?"

"First, I will tell you what I want, Captain Ohlsson."

"You are police?"

"No. I am a friend of the Llongo people. I am on a mission for them, to recover the sacred image."

From their expressions, he realized they knew what he was talking about and wouldn't need further explanations.

"I had no part in that damn thing," said the captain angrily. "I only took them aboard as passengers, Duke and Loka and that old fool."

"Sven!" shouted Sala. "Don't tell him!"

Sven raised his big hand, and she recoiled.

"I told you, keep that sweet mouth shut." His accent was gone now. He evidently could turn it on and off when it pleased him.

"Okay. Let's say that's the truth," said the Phantom, his voice still weak.

"Let's say?" shouted Sven. "I tell the truth. You better believe." His big hands grasped the Phantom's throat. The pressure was intense. The Phantom held his breath and waited. The hands relaxed. Sven was breathing hard.

"I can kill a man like that," he said.

"I believe that," said the Phantom quietly. Probably, he knew that from past experience. But this was no time to suggest that.

"Where did you take Duke and Loka?"

"Sven!" said the girl sharply. This time, the man swung at her, openhanded. She ducked the blow and fell backwards off the chest. Sven and Monkey-Face laughed. She was on her feet in a split second, grabbing the handiest object, a heavy brass candlestick. She went at Sven, swinging it. Still laughing, he caught her arm and shook the candlestick out of her hand. It hit the floor with a bang. Laughing, he lifted her into the air and held her in a bearhug. She tried to scratch at his bearded face, but he held both of her slim hands in one big paw, and covered her scarlet face with his big beard, kissing her passionately. The fight evidently stirred him up. She relaxed. He placed her back on the chest, seating her lovingly and carefully as if she might break, then turned back to his captive.

"Where were we?" he said. Monkey-Face cackled.

"Duke and Loka, where did you take them? Ivory-Lana?" That was the next port up the line, one of the *Moru Benga*'s usual calls. Sven stopped smiling. His face hardened.

"I've told you all I'm gonna tell you. Time you start talking now. I got you figured, man."

"How?"

"You're after that thing—that statue. Friend of the Llongo are you? Gukaka," he snapped, using an unprintable jungle epithet. "You're after that bloody thing yourself. You know it's worth mucho dinero, Sven."

"Any idea how mucho?"

"No, and I don't give a damn. I want nothing more to do with it—or them! And that goes for you, too," he snapped at Sala. She did not answer. He turned back to the Phantom. "Okay. Spill it, *mein freund*. Who are you? You'll never catch up with those two buckos. They're far gone."

"So is Old Murph," said the Phantom softly.

Both men reacted to that. Monkey-Face raised his pistol. Sven clenched his big fists.

"Never heard of him," he shouted.

"He was killed on your ship," said the Phantom softly.

"I had nothing to do with that," roared Sven.

"Who did?" Again, the soft voice.

"Nobody!" Sven was shouting as though into a storm.

"Sven, leeme finish the gukaka," said Monkey-Face, moving closer with his gun.

"No," roared Sven, pushing him away with a sweep of his arm. "What do you know about that, about Old Murph?"

"All I know is, he was murdered on your *Moru Benga*, Sven."

Sven's eyes popped with rage. His big hands reached for his captive's throat. It was the moment the Phantom was waiting for, when the captain's body would be between him and Monkey-Face's gun. As Sven bent over him, he brought his knees up sharply, catching Sven's chin. As the captain staggered back, the Phantom kicked up hard, kicking him in the jaw. Sven fell back toward Monkey-Face, who scrambled unsuccessfully to get out of the way. The big falling body hit him, and Monkey-Face was knocked off his feet. Within the same split second, the Phantom was up, scooping up Sala's knife from the floor only a few feet away. In the confusion, Sala started for the cabin door. Before she could reach it, the Phantom had sliced his ropes and reached her, pulling her back into the cabin.

By now, Monkey-Face was climbing out from under Sven and reaching for his gun, which had fallen to the floor. As his hand sought it, the Phantom's foot stamped on the hand. Monkey-Face howled. The Phantom picked up the pistol and pocketed it. Then he pushed Sala gently to the chest. All this had happened in a few seconds. He still had his hat on. He decided it was time to take it off.

As Sala stared in amazement, he removed his outer garments. The hooded, masked figure emerged. Her amazement turned to unreasoning terror. Who . . . what . . . was this? Monkey-Face sat against the wall, nursing his injured hand. He, too, stared uncomprehendingly. Sven groaned and mumbled. He had been knocked out briefly. He opened his eyes, rubbed his jaw, then sat up, to see the grim masked figure. His eyes widened. His big hands clutched together and sweat broke out on his forehead. Was it possible?

Captain Sven Ohlsson had never seen the Phantom. But he was a seaman. He had sailed all the seven seas, and wherever he went, he had always heard the tales . . . hundreds of stories told at the railing at night on a calm sea, told in the fo'c'sles of a dozen ships, told at sailors' bars. The legend every seaman knew and believed—the nemesis of pirates, the Ghost Who Walks, the Phantom.

As Sven stared, it all made sense to him. This stranger, who had handled those tough bouncers so easily. This man (man?) who could recover so quickly from the hard head-blow (had it hurt him at all?). This man who moved with inhuman swiftness, like the wind.

"You know me, Sven?" said the deep voice, no longer soft and weak.

Sven nodded in confusion. "You are ... Phantom ... ?"

Sala and Monkey-Face reacted to that. They too knew the legend, as did all who lived in this coastal world.

"Phantom?" said Sala softly. "Are you ... real?" she added, confused by the nighttime tales of her childhood.

"Captain Sven Ohlsson, you will tell me where Loka and Duke are. You will tell me about the murder of Old Murph. You will tell me this at once. My time is short. I am in a hurry. Is that clear?"

Sven nodded. His head was clearing. Whoever, whatever this man was, he was a real man. No ghost had kicked him in the jaw. He looked about casually. Sala's knife was close, on the little end table. The man was standing casually, hands on his hips. His eyes couldn't be seen behind the mask.

"Can I get up?" said Sven. The masked man nodded.

Sven got up slowly, as if in pain, then made a sudden quick move for the knife. His hand never reached it. Something hit him on the side of the jaw, like the kick of a mule (which he had once experienced). He crashed into the end table, and fell against the wall. He gasped, almost sobbed. He felt like his head had almost been, knocked off his neck. He opened his mouth slowly. Jaw broken? Felt like it. No, still worked ... barely.

"If you try that once more, I'll hit you hard," said the masked man. He was standing again, hands on hips as before. Had he actually moved? The others had seen him move—almost faster than the eye could follow. They also saw something else as Sven sat up against the wall and took his hand from his aching jaw.

"Sven! On your jaw!" said Sala. "Look in the mirror!"

There was a long mirror on the closet door at his side. He turned and stared at his face. On the jaw was a mark that had not been there before. It was a skull mark—a death's head. He rubbed at it. It wouldn't come off. Now he stared at the masked figure with unconcealed fear. He knew about that mark. He'd heard about it more than once. This was the proof of the pudding. This was it. He began to blubber. It was a strange sight, this big powerful bearded man, rubbing his jaw, trying to hold back his tears.

"It won't come off. Won't come off," he said, choking, sobbing.

The fabled death's head ring of the Phantom, always worn on his right fist, left its mark like a tattoo and was as difficult to remove. The sight of it not only frightened Sven. It seemed to stun him.

Monkey-Face sat equally fearful, his puckered countenance twitching, his eyes staring, spittle drooling from his mouth. Sala, less familiar with the legend, was shaken by the men's fear. Had she dared to trick the mysterious figure who now loomed like a giant before her. What would he do to her?

"I asked you to talk. Must I repeat my questions, Captain Sven Ohlsson?"

The bearded man shook his head and, rubbing his jaw, began to talk. First slowly, then rapidly.

Duke was an old buddy of his. They had shipped together more than once, fought together as mercenaries in more than one bush war. Drinking buddies, fighting buddies. Duke told him about this deal. Same old jungle statue could be sold for mucho dinero. How much? Plenty, Duke told him. He could trust his old buddy. Problem was to get it out of Bangalla fast, because police and Jungle Patrol were on the lookout for it. Why so much fuss? Because, Duke told him, the wogs (Duke's term for all dark-skinned people) being heathens, they worshiped the bloody thing.

Anyhow, Duke promised him twenty-five percent of the deal, if he'd get them up to a port where they could get a plane. This was a lot of trouble for Sven because he wasn't due to sail for another week. But he took off early for ol' Duke. Ol' Duke had a wog buddy, Loka. Sven knew Loka. A high flier, big gambler, liked the girls. Sven glanced at Sala at that point. She looked away. (The Phantom sensed here that Sven had taken Loka's girl away from him. Had this been part of the trouble? No, that turned out to be wrong.)

They came aboard at night, Duke, Loka, Sala, and Old Murph. Sven knew Old Murph from the Mawitaan bars. Everybody in Mawitaan knew Old Murph. The ship had barely gotten started when the wrangling started. It seems that though Old Murph had been with Duke when he snatched the statue, he hadn't realized it. This was easy to believe. Old Murph was always three sheets to the wind. He had been tipsy when he came up the gangplank, and he'd continued to drink. But the sight of the statue had upset him. He seemed to know a lot about it, and was insisting that they return it.

Sala nodded. That's the way it was.

After much arguing, Duke shut Old Murph in a cabin.

But after an hour or two, the old man got out. By this time, most of the ship's crew and passengers were asleep, including the captain. Only the man at the wheel and the first mate (Monkey-Face) were awake.

"Tell him what happened, Muggs," said Sven.

"I seen it," said Muggs, for that was Monkey-Face's name. "Old Murph got into Loka's cabin, got the statue, and started running with it on deck."

Sven explained: The old drunk was trying to get ashore. Loka ran out after him, yelling something about no man except a Llongo could touch it. "Right?" said Muggs. Sala nodded.

"That was afterwards," she said, correcting him.

"After what?" said the Phantom, his scalp beginning to tighten. Muggs went on.

"Old Murph, running, fell on the deck with the statue in his arms. This statue had long sharp horns and Old Murph fell on them, and that's what killed him. No man touched him," said Muggs in his squeaky voice.

"That's the way it was," said Sala.

The Phantom shivered. That Llongo curse again . . .

"I was asleep," Sven broke in. "Muggs came in and woke me up. When I got on deck, Duke was standing there with Loka and Sala. She was crying her eyes out. Old Murph was gone."

"Gone where?"

"Duke threw him overboard. Said he was dead. Had to get rid of the body, or we'd be blamed."

"That's all true," said Sala.

"Was he wearing a life vest?" asked the Phantom.

Muggs stared at him. How could he know that?

"He had one over his arm when he was running. Maybe he figured to swim ashore with the statue."

The Phantom meditated for a moment. That's how it was. It rang true. He'd seen the ship at dawn, about the time Old Murph had gone overboard.

"You didn't report this to the port authorities?" he said to Sven. The big man flushed.

"I'm a respectable sea captain. I got respectable business. I carry mail for Bangalla. Freight. Passengers. Back and forth. I want no trouble. None of this was my business. Not my fault."

This could be big trouble for all of them. The theft of a sacred religious image was bad enough. Murder was worse. In more civilized communities to the north and west, capital punishment was banned, frowned upon. Bangalla was an old-fashioned country. The ancient code was still in force. An eye for an eye, a tooth for a tooth. Murder was punished by hanging. There was no plea bargaining, no time off for good behavior, no pardons, when murder was involved. In Bangalla, the killer was hung. In Ivory-Lana, the killer was beheaded with an old-fashioned guillotine.

So, being charged with the murder of Old Murph could be fatal for any or all of them.

"Where did Duke and Loka leave ship?"

"Ivory-Lana."

"That is true," said Sala. "I wanted to go with them. Loka

wanted me to go. Duke wouldn't let me. He said I would be in the way. He made me come back on the ship."

In spite of his aching jaw, Sven grinned at that. He had evidently taken full advantage of the situation. The image had brought him luck—Sala.

"Wanted to go where? Where did they go?"

Sven and Sala hesitated. They looked at each other stubbornly. Sven folded his arms on his chest, signifying that he'd finished talking. The Phantom took one step toward him. His arms fell to his sides.

"London," he shouted.

"Where in London?"

Sven clenched his big fists and gritted his teeth, but he had to answer this masked figure who stood over him.

"I'm not sure where they went, exactly. Neither one knew London. I been there many a time. Duke asked me for a hotel. Not a sailor's dump, he said. He wanted something with class. I knew one pretty good one. Beresford Arms."

The Phantom gathered up his outer garments and walked to the door. The three watched him fixedly, like birds caught in the hypnotic stare of a serpent. He stopped at the door.

"If any of you have lied about any of this, I will come back. You will all be charged with the murder of Old Murph. You understand what that means."

All tried to protest at once. Sven's big voice carried over the others. "We told you what happened. We didn't kill him. He fell on that damn thing."

"I believe that he fell. But when Duke threw him overboard, he was not dead." They gasped. Their careful alibi—accidental death—was suddenly threatened.

"Impossible," said Sven. "He died. We were all witnesses."

"No," said the masked figure. "He died in my arms. I buried him at sea."

They looked at him dizzily. This was all weird. Where . . . how . . . ? But he wasn't answering any questions. Standing in the doorway, he said his final words to them.

"Perhaps, after he fell, he might have lived if he'd had immediate medical care. It's a question the judge would look into."

There were no juries in Bangalla, only hard-nosed judges.

Sven looked at Sala. Muggs stared at Sven. When they looked at the door, he was gone. Sven and Muggs rushed out on the deck. The ship rocked gently against the wharf. The ropes strained on the posts. Music and laughter tinkled from the nearby Blue Dragon. They peered into the fog. There was no one. Both men shivered and hurried back into the cabin.

CHAPTER 7

In its day, the Beresford Arms Hotel undoubtedly had had what Sven Ohlsson called "class." But that day was long past, though some faded, pre-World War I grandeur was still evident in the huge, dusty chandeliers that hung from the stained-glass ceilings over the large lobby. A broad marble staircase, soiled and cracked, with elaborate tarnished iron railings, swept up to the second floor. An ancient cagelike elevator slowly creaked up and down, shaking and groaning as though each trip was its last. All the metalwork was rusted. The carpeting in the wide, poorly lit halls was frayed. After countless coats of paint, the walls were dirty and cracked. A musty odor pervaded the halls and rooms, as though years had passed since fresh air had entered. A seasoned traveler knew even before getting beyond the front desk and the bored clerk that the beds would be lumpy, the linen soiled, the plumbing out of order. But even in this era of inflation and tight money, it was cheap. So travelers put up with it.

That's how Duke explained it to Loka, as the black man paced restlessly in their room. On the bureau, glowing like a jewel even in this sordid place, was the brilliant sacred image of the Llongo.

"How long do we stay in a miserable place like this?"

said Loka. Like all Llongo males, he was tall, broad-shouldered, muscular. He had a family resemblance to his handsome brother, Lamanda Luaga, but years of dissipation and disappointment had left their mark. His face was scarred and his mouth was mean.

Duke snorted and downed a shot of whiskey, then glared at his partner. "You kidding? You spent your life in mud huts. How old were you before you saw a real bed and inside plumbing?"

Duke was white, slim and tough. He'd gotten his nickname because of his smooth, aristocratic appearance. His hair was wavy and black, lightly flecked with gray. He'd shipped as a first mate and fought as a mercenary—an expert machine gunner. But he'd always preferred less violent activities, such as smuggling, drugs and jewels, con games involving fake gold and oil stocks and, when things were tough, a holdup or break-in robbery. Thus far, except for a brief stretch in Venezuela, he'd avoided arrest. He preferred what he called the "brainy jobs"— like this one.

Loka ignored the insults. Duke was too smart for him. Also, too quick with a knife.

"We got two, three million sitting there, and we sit in this dump. The beds are full of bugs."

"Listen, bucko, that thing is worth two, three million if and when we get a buyer. Right now we can't eat it. Not worth a red cent," said Duke, pouring another whiskey neat.

"We been here a week. You're the wise one. You know all about celling. That's what you been telling me," said Loka. "Where is this great buyer?"

Duke picked up the newspaper on the table and tossed it at Loka. On the back page there was a large picture of the image, and a news story about it. "It's hot, bucko. Hotter than a pistol. I got to pick my shots. By now, every dealer in town knows about this thing."

"Then why did we come here, to London? There are other places," said Loka.

"Because the dude I've picked is right here in London, bucko."

"You got a buyer? Who? Why didn't you say something?" said Loka excitedly.

"Remember the guys Old Murph told us about—the experts? I remembered one name. Helmsley. I been looking around. I found him."

"You talked to him?"

Duke took another shot of whiskey and reached for his hat. "I'm going now," he said, heading for the door.

"I'm going with you. I want to hear. No doublecross."

"And leave the thing sitting here for anybody to walk in and take? You crazy?" said Duke, meaning it.

"They got a safe downstairs. I saw the sign. We leave it in the safe," said Loka.

Duke nodded, anxious to get started. Loka placed the image in a carton, wrapped and tied it securely, then started for the door.

"Let me carry it," said Duke. Loka glared at him.

"Look, it can't get me, not while it's, in the box," said Duke, grinning, obviously not believing in the curse.

"We go," said Loka grimly. The curse was no joke to him.

The bored clerk behind the front desk lifted his eyebrows at the sight of the package.

"Awfully big," he said. "What are the contents?"

"Old china, teacups and like that," said Duke quickly. "Worth plenty, and breakable, bucko."

"Can't you leave it in your room?"

"And have one of those oxes you call chambermaids drop it? No thanks, bucko."

The clerk led them to a small room just off the front desk. He opened a large wall safe.

"Give it to me," he said.

Loka stared, looking dumbly at Duke.

"I said, breakable. Worth plenty. A couple months' wages, bucko, if you crack one little cup."

"You put it in. I want nothing to do with it," said the clerk quickly.

"Smart lad," said Duke, nodding to Loka. Loka placed the box inside the vault and they watched the clerk lock it.

"If anything is broken when we come back, you're responsible. Got that, bucko?" said Duke.

"Nobody's going to touch your precious teacups," the clerk said peevishly.

"What if he opens it?" said Loka as they walked outside.

"I think I fixed that," said Duke: "But, you never know. We got to take risks. We can't lug it through town."

They reached a small building that had a bank on the ground floor. Windows on the second floor were partly covered with brown velvet curtains.

"That's the place," said Duke.

"What kind of place? No name up there."

"This is no butcher shop, bucko. It's posh. Class."

In a small foyer, a neat sign on the wall read:

Cunningham & Helmsley
Antiquarians

They climbed the stairs and entered a small waiting room with paneled walls covered with paintings that, judged by their frames alone, looked expensive, and a thick red rug on the floor.

"Class," said Duke softly.

A woman seated behind a window opened the glass panel and looked inquiringly at them.

"Yes?" she said.

"We want to see Mr. Helmsley, please."

"Who shall I say is calling?"

"He doesn't know us. Just tell him two gentlemen from Bangalla."

"How do you spell that?"

Duke patiently spelled it. She closed the panel and reached for a phone. Loka looked admiringly at his partner. Duke looked and sounded like a gentleman. He was smooth. Brainy. In a moment, a small man with a neat dark mustache peered over the woman's shoulder, then opened the panel.

"You wish to see me? What about?"

He had the elegant upper-class-British accent that always impressed both Duke and Loka.

"We have something to sell, something you might be interested in seeing," said Duke, smooth and brainy. "Something rare, from Bangalla."

The man called Helmsley looked at him sharply. "Come in," he said.

There was a clicking sound as the door to the office unlocked. Duke opened it and they walked in.

They were in a large showroom. There were glass-enclosed shelves on the walls and rows of glass-topped cases. All the shelves and cases were locked. They contained various glittering objects: jeweled boxes, small statuary, framed paintings and drawings; all expensive-looking. They had only the briefest glimpse of all this as Mr. Helmsley led them quickly into an inner office. Duke, who was keenly observant, saw a small open panel on one wall from which eyes were watching. He had no doubt that the owner of the eyes also held a gun. Helmsley led them into the inner office, where a white- haired man sat behind a broad polished table. The man, like Helmsley, was immaculately dressed and looked like a banker.

"This is Mr. Cunningham, and you are . . . ?" said Helmsley.

"My name is Hanson, Fred Hanson. And this is Mr.

Murphy," he said, indicating Loka.

"You've brought something to sell?" said Mr. Cunningham.

"Can we speak in confidence?" said Duke.

The white-haired man glanced at his partner.

"That depends," he said.

"We have something of great value," said Duke, becoming uneasy with these stolid Englishmen. He thought quickly. He had nothing to lose here. He had broken no British laws. He took a newspaper from his pocket and displayed the picture story about the image. He tossed the paper on the polished table.

"This," he said.

Helmsley, the younger partner, reacted visibly. Cunningham, puzzled, picked up the paper and glanced at the story. Then he looked at Duke and Loka for a moment, his face remaining impassive.

"Are you saying that you have that object?" he said quietly.

"Let's say we know where it is," said Duke.

"Do you know that every police bureau in Europe has been alerted about that piece?" said Helmsley.

Loka looked at Duke in alarm, but Duke shrugged.

"So?" he said. "That doesn't matter."

"Doesn't matter?" said Cunningham. "No respectable dealer, museum or collector will touch it . . . not with a ten-foot pole."

"You're crazy, Cunningham," said Duke, suddenly angry. "It's worth millions."

"Granted, if it's genuine."

"It is genuine!"

"You have it?"

"We know where it is."

"You wish to sell that information?"

"Sell information. We wish to sell the image," said Duke heatedly.

"We are not interested. Good day, Mr. . . . . Hanson."

"Now just a minute, Cunningham. Helmsley, you know the thing, don't you. Tell him." Helmsley stared at him.

"I beg your pardon?"

Duke started to say, you saw it, you appraised it, but that involved Old Murph. That would complicate things.

"If you'd like to see it . . . " said Duke.

"No interest at all. Mr. Helmsley, will you see the . . . ah . . . gentlemen out?"

They followed Helmsley to the outer door.

"Can't you talk to him?" said Duke.

"Talk to him?" said Helmsley.

"You saw it. You know," said Duke.

"I beg your pardon. Saw it? Not likely. Good day, gentlemen."

They left confused, angry. Loka berated Duke all the way back to the hotel.

"Relax," said Duke. "He's not the only fish in the sea."

Helmsley returned to his partner.

"What did you think?" he asked.

"Phonies, con men, both of them," said Cunningham.

"You don't think they have the image?"

"The chances are a million to one against. They may have whipped up some imitation. Easy to do. I rather suspect they were trying to sell information which would turn out to be false."

"No doubt," said Helmsley, starting for the office door.

"Supposing—just supposing—they did smuggle the object out of Bangalla," Cunningham went on, glancing again at the newspaper on his desk. "Can you imagine the brouhaha in Parliament, in the Foreign Office, in Scotland Yard, if we or any other established outfit obtained it. I needn't remind you that foreign art treasures have become a risky matter."

"No question," said Helmsley, waiting impatiently at the door. Through the window, above the velvet cafe curtains, he could see the two men standing on the street corner, talking. As he started out of the office, his partner looked up from the paper.

"Odd they should come to us with this notion. When you were down there last year, didn't you see that object?"

"I was in Bangalla two years ago," said Helmsley carefully. "I saw several such idols. I may have seen that one."

"It seems to me I recall your talking about that odd curse. Sheba, Solomon, all that," said Cunningham, lighting a briar pipe.

Helmsley managed to chuckle.

"Quite possible. Every village has an idol that goes back to Adam and Eve." He started out the door.

"Helmsley, old boy, you didn't take those two seriously?"

"Hardly." He began to exit again.

"Will you call the police, or should I?"

He stopped. "Police?"

"It should be reported, just as a matter of form. The Yard or Foreign Office might want to look into it."

"Right," said Helmsley, and closed the door.

He ran through the elaborate showroom, grabbed his

bowler from a wall rack, muttered to the secretary about an appointment, and rushed down the stairs to the street. He saw the two men ahead, black and white, arguing as they walked. He sighed with relief and followed them at a safe distance, until they reached the Beresford Arms Hotel. He walked across the street and watched through the dirty lobby windows. He saw them stop at the front desk. The white remained there for a time while the black went out of sight. He returned with a large package and the two disappeared into the gloomy interior of the lobby.

A large package. Helmsley was breathing hard. The image —memories of a bumpy, dusty ride in Bangalla, that tipsy old guide (they had to take over the wheel), the glittering object, the visit to the President—it all came back in a flood. He bit his nails anxiously, plans racing through his mind. He rushed into a nearby phone booth, dialed, waited impatiently, then when a heavy voice answered, spoke excitedly into the mouthpiece, cupping it with his hand, meanwhile keeping watch on the front doors of the Beresford Arms Hotel across the street.

Completing the call, he went to a nearby pub and took a seat at the window where he could enjoy a pint of beer and keep his eye on the hotel. He wasn't going to let those two slip away. Not with that priceless thing.

CHAPTER 8

When they reached their room, Loka hurriedly unpacked the sacred image to make certain it was as he had left it. It was. Duke laughed at that. "That clerk wasn't about to break those teacups," he said.

"Now what?" said Loka.

"You think that Helmsley's the only fish in the sea? I got plenty of contacts in this town," said Duke.

He made a few phone calls. None of his contacts was in. He went through the phone book, looking under "Antiques" and "Antiquarians."

"See, dozens of them," he said.

"Dozens, ready to give us a million pounds for it?"

"How do I know until I try?"

"When will that be?"

"Too late today. Stores closed," said Duke, looking at his watch. "Start again tomorrow."

"I don't believe you've got any contacts. I don't believe you know what you're doing," said Loka.

"What makes you so smart?" snapped Duke.

"I'm an ignorant jungle boy, like you say. But I know this. When you got a hot thing like this, and want a million for it, you don't go looking in no phone book. You got to do better than that.

You said you had contacts!"

"I have, you stupid jungle bunny," said Duke. "Tomorrow."

Duke's overdefensive tone told Loka he was lying. Both men were coming to realize that in this complicated game of art robbery, they were amateurs. The brief visit to Cunningham & Helmsley had made them aware of it, but neither would admit it. They stared angrily at each other, then tried to pass the time with newspapers and girlie magazines. Their glances would flit for a moment to each other, to the glittering image on the bureau, then back to their reading. Their minds were working furiously. What now? Duke turned on the radio and they listened to a panel discussion on sanitation and garbage disposal, then the news. After reports about a disastrous hurricane in Central America, a flood in Italy, and famine in Asia—none of which was of the slightest interest to them—a local item riveted them in their chairs. It had the impact of a bolt of lightning from the ceiling.

"The following is from Scotland Yard," said the announcer in his condescending voice. "An art object valued at over a million pounds, stolen from its tribal owners in Bangalla, is believed to be in London. The art object, which has received considerable publicity recently, is known as the sacred image of the Llongo, a Bangalla people. It is described as a two-headed bull, made of jade, encrusted with enormous jewels—diamonds, rubies and emeralds. Legend has it that this object was given to the Biblical King Solomon by the Queen of Sheba. According to Scotland Yard, an eminent local art dealer whose name has been withheld was approached by two men who wished to sell the object. Their names are also withheld. They are described as follows: one white man, over six feet, dark hair, trim beard. The other one, black, clean-shaven, also about six feet tall, with a Bangalla accent. If anyone has knowledge of this pair, kindly report to Scotland Yard."

Duke and Loka stared at each other, then at the radio. Both felt as though a searchlight had suddenly turned on them, exposing them to the world.

"That damn Helmsley. Knew I shouldn't trust him," said Duke.

"They don't know our real names," said Loka.

"I gave them phonies—Hanson and Murphy," said Duke.

"Then we're safe," said Loka.

"Safe, stupid? Hear that description? One white, one black. Bangalla accent! How many pairs like that in London?"

"Many, maybe," said Loka hopefully.

"None! We got to split up."

"How do you mean, split up?"

"Separate. We're too easy to spot together. Get that through your thick head. They're looking for us. Courts are tough here. And there's extradition. Could be a murder rap in Mawitaan. Old Murph."

"We didn't kill him."

"Who'll believe that? No good, Loka. As long as I stay with you, we're in trouble. We got to split up. And you've got to hide out"

"Me hide? Why me?" said Loka. "Why not you?"

"I'm one white man among millions. You're black, stupid. You've got Bangalla written all over you. Every time you open your mouth. That accent. You're too easy to spot."

Duke put on his coat and hat and stood by the image.

"Clear out of this hotel. Find another place. Tomorrow I'll make contacts. We'll have a meeting place. Tomorrow night, midnight, down by the wharfs, White Bear Lines."

"White Bear Lines?" said Loka, becoming frantic.

"Some foreign ship line. Got a big white bear on the building. Ask anybody. Got that?"

Loka nodded dumbly, sweating and anxious.

"You won't doublecross me, Duke. If you do, I find you, I kill you," he shouted, suddenly furious.

"Right, right," said Duke. "I'm going now."

He was standing by the bureau. Loka grabbed his arm. "Duke, don't leave me. I don't know where to go. We got to stay together."

Duke shoved him away so roughly Loka lost his balance and fell to one knee.

"No, black and white. Too easy to spot. I told you. I can't trust you with this. You're too dumb to live. I'm taking it with me." And Duke grabbed the shining image.

Caught by surprise, Loka stared in amazement.

"No, Duke, no, you can't," he shouted as Duke headed for the door.

"I'm keeping this. You'd lose it, you stupid jungle bunny!" said Duke from near the door.

"No, that's mine!" Loka shouted. He dove at Duke, tackling him at the knees. Duke crashed to the floor with the image in his arms. He yelled with pain, groaned, tried to get to his feet, collapsed. Sitting on the floor, Loka stared at his friend, then touched him. Duke wasn't, moving. He wasn't breathing. The sharp horns of the sacred image were stuck in his chest.

Loka shook with fear as the full impact of this event became clear. Duke, an outsider, had touched the sacred image. He was dead. He had fallen on the horns. The image had killed him. It didn't matter how it happened—he was dead because of the image.

With trembling hands, he pulled the image from Duke's

body. Blood was forming a pool on the faded carpet. Now Loka realized the gravity of the situation. He was alone in this room with a corpse. He could be held for murder. Nobody would believe his story. He had to move, get out, with his priceless image.

He hurriedly packed it into the carton, tossed his few personal effects into his bag and went to the door. Duke hadn't moved. It was hard to believe he was dead. He had been so violently alive only minutes before. Loka looked about the room. The window shades were drawn. No one had seen. He listened carefully for sounds of voices or running feet. All was quiet. He peered out into the dim corridor. Empty. Good. No one had heard. Without a backward look, he quickly locked the door, then went to the antique elevator. He pressed the button impatiently, then saw the elevator was already rising from the lobby floor, probably with passengers. He didn't wait to be seen, but rushed down the broad staircase.

Two men were standing at the front desk, talking to the bored clerk. One was Helmsley. The other was heavyset, wearing a derby, a checkered suit, pink shirt, red tie with a large diamond stickpin. He removed a cigar from his lips to belch. As he spoke in a strong cockney accent, he belched several times. His florid complexion indicated he was a drinker. Probably the cause of the belch. They were inquiring about two guests in the hotel—a Mr. Hanson and a Mr. Murphy. The clerk shrugged. No such names were registered.

"You must be mistaken," said Helmsley.

"I am not mistaken," said the clerk. "We have no Hanson, no Murphy."

"Maybe we've got the names wrong," Helmsley replied, "One is black and the other white."

The clerk's eyes flickered with recognition at that, but he shook his head.

"We can't give out information unless you have the names of the parties. Rules," he said.

The man with the derby took out a large bank note.

"We don't care about the names. Just the room number," he said, waving the money. The clerk looked at it with bright eyes. It was equal to a day's wages for him. He smiled, took the money, and in the same moment, looked toward the stairs, attracted by the sound of footsteps.

"There's one of them now," he said, pocketing the money.

Breathing hard, his eyes glazed, Loka paid no attention to the men at the desk. His hands were full, the box under one arm, the bag in his other hand. He went out swiftly through the hotel doors. The two men followed immediately after him.

"Taxi, taxi," Loka called loudly as he moved to the curb. Several cabs were parked nearby. As one of them started up, Loka's arms were grasped. Helmsley on one side, the heavyset man on the other.

"We're going your way, Mr. Murphy. We'll give you a lift," said Helmsley. Loka stared at him in recognition.

"No," he said. "No."

"Yes," said the man with the derby, whose name was Bolt. He had a gun in his coat pocket, and he pressed against Loka. "Get in and shut up," said Bolt.

Loka stared at the florid face, at the hard gray eyes of the stranger, and he knew without being told. This was a killer. Loka did as he was told. He shut up, and got in. The two men sat on either side of him as he clutched his box on his lap, and the cab drove off.

CHAPTER 9

As the Phantom boarded the plane at the Mawitaan airport, it was with more than the usual excitement he felt when starting on a mission. This London-bound plane would have a stopover at Orly Airport in Paris. He cabled this to Diana in Paris, asking her to meet him at the airport for a quick visit during the stopover. He wasn't certain he would see her, but he had high hopes. There was a brief argument as he started up the plane stairs with Devil on a leash.

"You can't take that dog aboard, sir," said the stewardess, a pretty blond girl in a miniskirt.

"He's not a dog," said the Phantom. He'd been through this before. "He's a wolf."

The girl stared at the long teeth and pale blue eyes. She turned away and came back with a man in trim uniform, an airline official.

"What seems to be the difficulty," he said brightly.

"No difficulty. I've bought a seat for my animal. I'd like him with me."

"A wolf?" said the official with a toothy grin. "Wild animals are not permitted aboard, and must be crated, with special permission, as freight." He opened a pamphlet and showed the Phantom the regulation.

"There it is, in black and white. No wild animals," he said

triumphantly while two stewardesses looked on.

The Phantom sighed. It was always the same routine.

"He's not a wild animal. He's tame and trained, perfectly. Does your regulation say anything about that?" he said patiently.

The official grinned at the two stewardesses, who smiled. Then he turned to this troublesome passenger, and spoke as to a child.

"Sir, I read the rules. You cannot go on the plane with the animal," he added firmly.

"You've shown me no rule pertaining to a tame, trained wolf," said the Phantom quietly. "I would have no objection to your freight section, if you had modern facilities there like other airlines. But I know that neither the air pressure nor temperature are properly controlled in there. At thirty-five thousand feet, this would kill or severely injure my animal. I refuse to let this happen." The Phantom took a step toward the official, and his voice was cold and deep. "I have paid his passage. He will not bother other passengers. He will board with me."

The man looked into the dark sunglasses that revealed nothing of the eyes behind them. The deep cold voice seemed to come out of a well or a tomb. His knees trembled. His voice quavered.

"I cannot take any responsibility for this," he said shrilly.

"I will take all responsibility. Thank you."

He walked up the stairs with the wolf on its leash. The stewardesses stared at the official. He flushed, shrugged his shoulders, washing his hands of the business, and walked away. The stewardesses looked at his retreating figure in amazement. Throughout the company, this man was known as C.S. He lived by the rules, and was a petty tyrant to his underlings, or any confused passenger who broke petty rules.

"C.S. was scared to death," said the blonde.

"So was I," said the redhead. "That one is something!"

During the flight, "that one" continued to be "something." For one thing, he refused to remove his hat and coat, wearing them throughout the flight. His wolf sat next to him, its gray head rising as high as a man's. Other passengers craned their necks and made special trips to the washroom to observe this pair. When lunch was served, he ordered and obtained raw hamburger for the animal. "He usually catches his own meat," the passenger, a Mr. Walker, informed the enchanted stewardesses who vied with each other to serve him. A few people approached the seat to chat and satisfy their curiosity. But he pulled his hat over his forehead and pretended to sleep. He was daydreaming about Diana and wondering if she would meet him at Orly. She would. She did.

She was waiting at the gate as he strolled from the plane with Devil on a leash. She leaped up, threw her arms about his neck, delivered a quick kiss, then was on her knees, embracing Devil. The wolf knew her at once and licked her flushed cheek.

"Oh, I am so glad to see you, both of you," she shouted happily. Diana was a quiet girl and did not usually shout. This was a special moment. He lifted her to her feet.

"Let me look at you."

She faced him, smiling happily. She was even more beautiful than he had remembered. As usual, she was dressed to perfection, perhaps even more than usual for this meeting. She wore a trim suit, high-style French couture, a bright yellow scarf that set off her wavy mane of black hair.

"I've only a short time here before the plane leaves. Let's have coffee," he said.

Diana smiled and glanced at a suitcase at her side.

"I'm taking the weekend off. I'm going with you," she said.

For a moment, he was delighted, overwhelmed. A whole weekend together! Then a sober second thought.

"Diana, I'm on a serious mission. It might be dangerous. It involves men who may be killers."

"But I told them at the office I would be in London for the weekend. It's all arranged," she said.

"I have to move fast. It might be dangerous," he said. "If it is, I don't want you involved."

"No reason for me to get involved," she said, smiling. "London is a big place. While you are doing what you must do, I can go to some museums or matinées. They're having a wonderful season in London."

"Well, I suppose it'd be all right," he said doubtfully.

"Then it's settled. Tell me you think it's wonderful."

"It's marvelous," he said, laughing and put his arm around her shoulder. "Why try to argue with you? I knew you'd win."

Back on the plane, she sat next to him while Devil curled up at their feet. When the two stewardesses passed by to offer them cocktails or tea (they took tea) the girls looked at Diana with unconcealed envy.

He told her about Rex and Guran and Hero and all her friends in the Deep Woods, where she had visited several times. He also told her about the sacred image of the Llongo. She had read about its disappearance and was fascinated that this was his mission. Diana was an old friend of Lamanda Luaga and had served as nurse on a UN medical team that he headed before he became President of Bangalla. The fact that this disappearance, engineered by his brother, might affect his career angered her. She shared the Phantom's admiration for their friend.

An hour later, they left Heathrow Airport and were in a taxi headed for London.

"I've got one lead I must look into now. I'll drop you at this museum. If I'm not at the front doors at closing time, check in at the Waldorf. I'll get in touch with you there."

The taxi stopped at an old building, the Victoria and Albert Museum. He kissed her quickly. She pressed his hand. She was no longer smiling. "You said this could be dangerous. Please be careful." She kissed him, then taking her suitcase, left quickly.

"To the Beresfordt Arms Hotel," he told the driver.

As his taxi reached the place, he could not know that another taxi, carrying Loka and the two men, had left only a few minutes before. He entered the lobby with Devil on the leash and went to the front desk. The bored clerk was deep in a racing form and finished his reading before looking up. He saw the big man in sunglasses, and as he stood up, he saw the animal.

"We don't allow pets here," he said.

"I don't want a room. I'm looking for two men staying here."

"Names?"

"Would Duke and Loka help?"

"None such registered here."

"One is black, one is white."

The clerk studied that for a moment. He'd just had that question a short time earlier, and had been well paid for his answer. Why all the interest in those two?

"Can't release information about guests unless you have the name," he said stiffly, the image of another generous tip forming in his mind.

The stranger put a heavy hand on his frail shoulder.

"This is a criminal matter. It's best you do not obstruct justice," he said flatly.

The clerk stared, his vision of money dissolving at once. "Oh, I didn't know. Are you . . . ?"

"Yes, I am. What room?"

"Hanson and Murphy. Three forty-nine. One of them, the black, just left—with friends, I guess."

"I'll want to know more about those friends later."

"Listen," said the clerk, leaning over the counter as the man started off. "We don't want any trouble. This is a decent law-abiding place."

"Good. Keep it that way."

The man did not wait for the elevator. He and the big shaggy dog bounded up the stairs. The clerk wondered if he should call his boss, the proprietor. No, better wait to see if it amounted to anything. The boss didn't like to be bothered.

The Phantom reached Room 349 and listened at the door. No sounds. His keen, jungle-trained hearing could pick up the slightest movement. Nothing. He tried the door. It was locked. He leaned against it, then used his entire weight to spring the old lock. The door opened. He saw the body on the floor at once, entered quickly with Devil and shut the door behind him.

The man was dead. From the description he'd gotten on the *Moru Benga*, this must be Duke. He examined him quickly for the cause of death and found the twin wounds. Like Old Murph's. For a moment, his mind reeled. The sacred image?

"One of them, the black, just left—with friends, I guess," the clerk had said. One had left, and one had stayed here. The white one. The Phantom picked up the phone. The strained voice of the clerk answered.

"Get a doctor up here. A man's dead. You'll need a death certificate."

The clerk gasped and hung up. The Phantom looked through the room. There was one duffel bag, the sort seamen use. Duke's. One razor, one toothbrush in the bathroom. A can of powder spilled on the floor. One sock hanging out of a drawer. Someone had left in a hurry. Loka. There was a knock on the door. He opened it. A man wearing a white jacket was buttoning it with one hand. In his other hand was a black leather bag.

"I'm the house doctor. My office is downstairs," he began. He saw the body on the floor, and quickly knelt by its side, using a stethoscope. He saw the blood and found the wounds.

"Still warm," he said. "This man's been dead less than an hour." The Phantom nodded. "You see it happen?" The Phantom shook his head. The door opened. A policeman walked in followed by the wide-eyed clerk.

"That's our doctor. That's the man I told you about," said the clerk.

"You reported this?" The Phantom nodded.

"He's dead. Stabbed," said the doctor.

"You see it happen," asked the policeman.

"No. But I believe I know how it happened. Those two wounds on the chest—"

"Cause of death," said the doctor.

"—made by the jade horns of the sacred image of the Llongo."

"What?" said the policeman.

"It's an ancient image. Only the Llongo people of Bangalla can touch it, or so they believe. This man, no Llongo, must have touched it. It's an ancient curse," he said, knowing how his words must sound to these men who stared at him.

"Crazy," muttered the clerk.

"We'll get into all that later," said the policeman as he wrote in his notebook. "Name, please?"

"Walker."

"Residence?"

"Bangalla."

The officer looked up from his- writing at that. "That's where the deceased and the other man, the black, came from?" The Phantom nodded. The clerk must have told the policeman about Loka.

"Did you know the black man, called Murphy?" The Phantom shook his head. He had never met Loka. "Or the deceased?" Negative, again.

"When you called downstairs, this man was dead?"

"Had to be," said the doctor. "Had been dead an hour when I came, right after that."

"I have to call the morgue. Then you come with me to the station," said the policeman, walking to the phone.

"Sorry, I can't go with you."

The policeman turned and looked at him in surprise.

"I must find the other man—Murphy—and the image," said the Phantom.

"Kind of you to do our job, sir. We'll handle that." The policeman looked at the clerk. "You call the morgue. I want to leave now with this witness."

"Sorry, officer," said the Phantom as he went toward the door. "But I haven't time now." The policeman moved quickly to block the door, held the Phantom's arm, and gripped his night stick firmly.

"You'll come with me. You're a material witness. You may be more into this than you've said—coming from the same place as the deceased and the missing man," said the policeman.

"I understand you bobbies carry no firearms. Correct?"

"Correct."

"I do," said the Phantom, pulling away from the policeman's grip and at the same time drawing a shining automatic from an inner pocket. "Stand over there. You too, Doctor."

"Obey him," said the doctor. "He is pathological."

The Phantom smiled. "I know it sounds crazy—the sacred image—but it's a complicated story, too long to tell now."

As he spoke, he ripped the telephone cord from the wall. "I'd prefer to let you and your colleagues take care of this, officer, but I must handle my part of it. It involves an ancient law of another people, not your law, not your people." Then he grasped the clerk's arm. The frail man trembled at his touch. "Come with me," said the Phantom, pulling him to the door.

"Why, what are you going to do?" said the man shrilly.

"I'm not going to hurt you. I want to talk to you. Have you got your passkey?"

The man nodded, taking a key on a chain from his pocket.

"Sir, you're making a mistake. You can't get away. We'll find you," said the policeman.

"Possible, but unlikely," said the Phantom. He took the clerk out into the corridor and quickly locked the door, then moved down the hall with the man.

"Which room opens onto a fire escape?"

"All of them. Fire laws," said the clerk weakly.

"Open this one," he said, stopping at a door.

The clerk looked at him indignantly. "It's occupied," he said.

The Phantom shook his arm roughly. "Open it!"

The clerk gulped and quickly opened the door. A middle-aged woman, hair in curlers, sat up in bed and stared at the two men and a dog as they rushed through her room toward the window.

"How dare—how dare you!" she screamed. "I'll report this to the clerk." She reached frantically for her bedside phone.

"I am the clerk," he said, as the Phantom shoved him through the window onto the fire escape.

"Mr. Phipps! What is the meaning . . . ?" she began.

"Sorry to disturb you, madam," said the other man. A big furry animal leaped after him, and they were gone. She looked at the phone, then at the window. There was no one to call.

The Phantom reached the roof with the clerk.

"Talk fast," he said to the frightened man. "When that black left, did he carry a package?"

"Yes . . . yes . . . a box. Tea set, I think."

"Tea set?"

"This morning they left it in our safe. Said it was valuable tea cups and all."

"Did you see the tea cups?"

"Oh no. We never pry into valuables left by guests."

"You said the black man left with two friends. Who were they?"

"I don't know. Maybe not friends. They didn't know his name."

"How do you know that?"

"They came to the desk, like you, asking about a black and a white man. Just then the black man came down with the package. They took him off in a cab."

"Took him off? By force?"

"Oh, I couldn't say as to that, sir. It just seemed odd, not knowing his name. Then going off like that."

"You watched?"

"Through the window."

"Describe the two men."

"Never saw them before. One was—a gentleman, I guess. Smallish. Neatly dressed. Bond Street, I'd say. Little mustache, bowler."

"The other one."

"More of a toff. Big. Flashy type. More like a gambler, race-track type, loud clothes, high color."

"Anything else about that one?"

The clerk looked embarrassed. "A peculiarity. A steady sort of belching, you might say. Rather uncouth."

The policeman broke open the door of 349. He rushed out with the doctor and saw an open door several rooms away. He looked in. The woman was still in bed.

"Excuse us, madam. Did you see a man and a dog go by?"

"Did I see them? They came into my room. The man and Mr. Phipps."

"Where did they go?"

She pointed to the open window. "Out the window, up the fire escape."

The policeman rushed to the window. "Begging your pardon, ma'am," he said, climbing out onto the fire escape.

"Not at all," she said tartly. "Why don't you stay and direct traffic?"

On the roof. Devil gave two warning barks. A moment later, the policeman's head appeared over the ledge at the lire escape.

"You're under arrest," he shouted, waving his night stick as he climbed onto the roof.

While questioning the clerk, the Phantom had surveyed the surroundings. Now, with Devil at his heels, he turned, ran to the far edge of the roof and leaped over a twenty-foot gap to the roof of the building. Devil sailed over after him. He continued on without stopping, across the next roof, jumping to another level, then out of sight behind a water tank. The policeman and the clerk walked to the edge of the roof where he had jumped. An alley was three floors below.

"Going to jump after him?" said the clerk, relaxing after all the excitement, feeling safe enough now to grin.

"Me. I'm no blooming acrobat," said the policeman. He returned down the fire escape, the clerk with him. They went through the same window they had used before. The lady was starting to get out of bed. She immediately got under the covers.

"Excuse me, please," said Mr. Phipps, the clerk.

"Hope you don't mind, ma'am," said the policeman.

"Mind? Might as well have my bed on the sidewalk. Mr. Phipps, prepare my account. I'm leaving."

"Please don't be hasty, Mrs. Murgatroyd. This is a police matter. There's been a murder."

"Oh my God," said Mrs. Murgatroyd.

Downstairs at the front desk, the policeman made his report.

"White, armed, sunglasses when last seen, over six feet, fifteen stone . . . yes, a big one . . . gray hat, checkered topcoat, big gray dog, shaggy like a wolf. Still in vicinity. The black man, last seen wearing brown jacket, blue trousers, just under six feet, short hair, Bangalla accent . . . B-a-n-g-a-l-l-a. Where is that, who knows? Down there someplace." He hung up.

"We'll need a statement from you, Mr. Phipps."

"I'm on duty here until midnight."

"Come tomorrow. This is an odd one, for sure. We'll want your description of the two the black man went out with."

Mr. Phipps nodded. "As best I can remember," he said.

A black truck pulled up at the curb. Two men in white coats climbed out and entered the hotel, one carrying a stretcher.

"Hello, boys. The body's in three forty-nine."

They nodded and went up the stairs without a word. Phipps shivered. "Will you find him?" he said.

"They'll both be easy. Men from the districts are already surrounding this area. House-to-house search. He's not likely to get away. He'll help us find the others."

As the policeman walked to the door, Phipps trotted at his side, excited and curious.

"If the man with the gun—if he is part of the gang, why would he call down . . . you know, report it?"

"Mr. Phipps, if you'd apprehended as many perpetrators as I have in my time, you'd come to know that the criminal mind is hard to fathom. Why did he do it? A bluff? Playing innocent or . . ." He paused and grinned. "You heard all that about the curse. A bit dotty, I'd say."

"A lunatic?"

"More of them walking the streets than you'd believe."

Mr. Phipps shivered. It was all like a show on the telly. "What do you make of it all, officer?" he asked on the sidewalk.

"A falling-out among thieves. A quarrel over the loot. Happens every day. Tea cups, indeed." He chuckled.

"How would I know the contents of the box? We never pry into guests' valuables," said the clerk, flushing.

"A fine rule," said the policeman, his blue eyes twinkling. "Good day, Mr. Phipps."

He walked off chuckling. "Tea cups."

The Phantom moved across a dozen roofs until he
reached one that overlooked a side street. Peering over the edge,
he saw a police car pull up at the curb. Several men, obviously
plainclothesmen, stepped out. A uniformed policeman walked over
to them. They conferred for a moment, then separated. Probably
searching for him. He'd been in this situation before. Working
outside the law to catch lawbreakers. He would have preferred to
let the law take over, drop out of it, and spend the weekend with
Diana. But this was impossible, He had his duty to the Llongo and
to Lamanda Luaga. He couldn't go back on his word. And it would
be difficult to explain his presence in London or to avoid being
implicated in the murder in Room 349. The three there—policeman,
doctor, and clerk—had thought his quick explanation crazy. Others
would have the same reaction. He couldn't blame them. But it meant
that he had to work alone and quickly. He had to find Loka, the
"toff" who belched and the dapper Bond Street type. Not much to go
on. He did have one more vague lead. An art dealer named Helmsley.
That might lead to something.

He thought about Diana. The museum would be closing
about now. He wouldn't be there. She would go on to her hotel and
wait. And wait alone. He couldn't leave now. Had to wait until dark,
wait for a chance to escape from this area that was being searched,
and find a hiding place for Devil. Staying with the gray wolf made
him too easily identifiable. He sat at the edge of the roof and waited.
As soon as it was dark, he would move.

After hours of examining the costumes and furniture of the
Victorian Age, and having tea and scones three times, and waiting in
the front lobby until closing time, Diana left the museum and went
to the hotel as planned. There she asked for a quiet first-floor room,
preferably in the back of the hotel. She was given such a room in this
quiet, well-run old hostelry. She showered, leaving the bathroom
door open so as not to miss hearing the phone . . . which did not
ring. Then she sat in a chair and tried to read. But she was nervous,
worried about him.

Though she had known him ever since they were children
during his school years in Clarksville, and though she had visited his
shadowy jungle many times, his amazing background and unique
life were still a tantalizing mystery to her. What other girl on earth
had a Phantom lover like this one —a man known and loved and
believed immortal by millions? A sweetheart who was at once the
Keeper of the Peace, the Guardian of the Eastern Dark (whatever
that meant—he'd told her, but she had forgotten) and the Ghost Who

Walks. That was the name that thrilled her. The Ghost Who Walks. She whispered it softly.

This wasn't the weekend she'd hoped for. Danger, killers. She felt a sudden panic. What if something had happened to him? Then she pictured the powerful hands, the firm jaw, the force that radiated from that steely body—-no, no one could hurt him. He would take care of himself. The Ghost Who Walks. She dozed off. The phone rang.

CHAPTER 10

Loka sat tensely clutching the box and staring defiantly at the three men. They were in the basement game room of a small house. There was a pool table and a bar loaded with bottles. Bolt straddled a chair, leaning on the back of it as he alternately gulped straight whiskey and puffed and relit and puffed a cigar. Helmsley sat at the side sipping a scotch and soda. The third man, Gyp, drank wine from a water glass. He was short, muscular, olive-complexioned, a gold ring in his ear. He was a Gypsy, hence the name. Between a gulp and a puff. Bolt laughed derisively.

"That's your story? The thing in the box killed your partner?"

"It was not in the box. He tried to take it," said Loka for the fifth time.

"We heard you," said Bolt. "He tried to take it, and you stabbed him and left him dead."

Loka's eyes almost popped with rage.

"I did not kill Duke! The image killed him. The curse!" he shouted at the top of his voice.

Helmsley got up in alarm.

"Keep your voice down, for God's sake," he said anxiously.

"Let him yell," said Bolt. "Nobody'll hear him. The place is soundproof." He pointed to the walls and ceiling. They were covered with acoustical panels. "It's not the first time somebody yelled down here. Louder than that. Much louder. Won't be the last," he said lazily. The implication of torture was clear. Gyp grinned knowingly, revealing a set of gold teeth, while Helmsley looked uncomfortable. He was obviously unused to such company.

"Okay, Loco, let's have it straight," Bolt began.

"Loka!" said Loka angrily.

"Loco, Loka, so you didn't kill your buddy. The thing did. Right?" Loka nodded vigorously. "Let's say we buy that. Do the coppers buy that, Gyp?"

The Gypsy snorted. "Never."

"You're not in your lousy bush now, wherever it is. You're in England. A black kills a white—we don't like that here."

"I didn't, I didn't!" shouted Loka.

Helmsley shuddered at the loud voice, at the threatened violence. He snapped on the small radio at his side. "News time," he said. "Let's see if they have anything on it yet."

The announcer was talking about the weather. Rain, for a change. Loka looked angrily at Helmsley.

"How did the radio, the papers, know the image was here —with a black man and a white man?" he finished, mimicking the broadcaster.

"My senior partner, Cunningham, reported to the police as soon as you and your buddy left our showrooms," said Helmsley.

"Shh," said Gyp. "Listen."

It was an item about the Beresford Arms. Murder was still news in London.

". . . a visitor, said to be a seaman, one Fred Hanson, was stabbed to death in the venerable Beresford Arms Hotel. Police believe the name is an alias. His roommate, a Bangallan black man named Murphy"—the announcer chuckled, Loka sat up rigidly—"also believed to be an alias, is sought by the police as the alleged killer. There was a bizarre chase over the rooftops as police pursued an alleged accomplice and a big shaggy dog. A manhunt is on in the area for the alleged killer and the unnamed alleged accomplice, and the alleged shaggy dog. Robbery was the motive, police state, and—" Helmsley snapped off the radio.

"Who was the man with the dog?" said Bolt. "Who else was with you?"

"Nobody. Just me and Duke . . . and the image," he said, clutching the box tighter.

"You're holding out. Who else is in on this," said Bolt, getting up from his chair. Loka looked up at him with frightened eyes.

"Nobody else. I know no man with a dog."

Bolt swung, hitting him with the back of his hand. The force of the blow toppled Loka off the stool onto the floor. He sat there, bent over the box.

"No man, no dog, no man, no dog," he wailed.

Bolt kicked him hard in his side. Loka yelped. Helmsley took Bolt's arm. The big man was in a fury.

"Easy, Bolt," he said. "We need this man."

"For what? He's got the thing. We take it. Who needs him?"

The big man looked angrily at Gyp. The dark-skinned man pulled a long knife from his belt.

Helmsley trembled but clenched his fists.

"I'm a businessman. I won't be involved in any violence."

That amused Bolt. "Some businessman—owing me ten thousand quid."

"My business is art, not race horses. They are my pleasure, not my vocation."

"And not your profit," said Bolt. "Give my one reason why we need this miserable scum?"

"If we want a million pounds for what he has in that box," he began.

"You said two million," said Bolt quickly.

"Could be two million, even three. The object is intrinsically valuable, but not to that extent. Its antiquity and its authenticity are the factors that increase its value perhaps ten times. That's why we need him. He is Llongo."

Helmsley's upper-class tones soothed the cockney Bolt. Whatever his politics, the average Britisher has a mystical adoration for his superiors, and the accent of the high-born fills him with reverence and delight. So it was with Bolt. He vaguely understood such terms as antiquity and authenticity, but was too embarrassed to ask for further explanations. It was with such social graces that the British held one-quarter of the earth for so long.

"Okay, he stays. Let's see the thing," said Bolt. Gyp regretfully sheathed his knife.

"Yes, Loka, open the box," said Helmsley, now in control. Loka got to his feet, casting aggrieved looks at Bolt and Gyp. He'd seen the Gypsy's knife. He untied the cords binding the box, then carefully removed the image, placing it on the pool table. The men stared. Helmsley went to it quickly. He had a small jeweler's glass. He put it to his eye and closely examined the glittering statue.

"That's it, that's it," he said excitedly.

"Crazy thing. Are those real sparklers?" said Bolt.

"Real."

"Worth two million quid?"

"To the right party, yes," said Helmsley.

"You can find the right party?" said Gyp.

"That is my business."

"I want my share. Half," said Loka.

Bolt exploded with laughter.

"Half? You are demented, man."

"That was the split for Duke and me. Half," said Loka stubbornly.

"There were only two of you," said Helmsley. "Now there are four."

"I'll see you get your share. All that you've got coming to you," said Bolt with a wink at Gyp. "Let me see that thing," he added, reaching for the image. Loka moved like a flash between him and the pool table.

"No you cannot touch it," he exclaimed. Bolt shoved him aside impatiently, but he grabbed his arm. "No, you cannot." No one told Bolt what to do. His heavy fist landed on Loka's jaw. Loka fell to his knees. "You fool, if you touch that, you will die, at once!"

Bolt's hard eyes narrowed. "What's that black bastard trying to say to me, Helmsley?"

"It's about the curse," said Helmsley hesitantly.

"What curse?" demanded Bolt. Gyp's eyes widened. He knew about curses.

"Tell him, Loka," said Helmsley.

"Only one of my people, the Llongo, may touch. If anyone not of my people touches, he dies. It kill him."

Bolt rumbled with laughter, but his eyes remained narrowed.

"It is the truth," said Loka, getting to his feet. "On the ship, Old Murph tried to take it. It killed him. Duke tried to take it. It killed him. I saw both. It is the curse."

"Hogwash," said Bolt. "Pure hogwash."

Helmsley smiled. "Go ahead and prove it's hogwash, Bolt. Pick it up."

Bolt was a gambler. Luck, good and bad, was part of his life. He looked at the intense face of Loka. Then at Gyp, whose lips wore tight and who shook his head. Then at Helmsley, who smiled but whose eyes were too bright. Then at the weird glittering object.

"Yeah, who cares about such kid stuff? Not me," he rumbled and walked to the bar for another whiskey. The men exchanged glances. None dared to comment. "Who'll you sell this to, Helmsley?" said Bolt gruffly from the bar.

"I've many clients. I'll go over my list today and make a few calls," said Helmsley.

"Does your partner, what's-his-name, know about this?"

"Of course not," said Helmsley quickly. "He'd kill the deal. He's not going to know about it."

"Okay. I've had enough of this. I'm going to the track," said Bolt. "You stay here, bushman. Gyp, don't let him or it out of this room. Got it?"

"Got it," said Gyp, showing his gold teeth.

Helmsley and Bolt walked to the door together. Loka followed them.

"I want my share," he said.

"Don't worry, boy. ..You'll get what's coming to you," said Bolt. They closed the door. Gyp took a key from his pocket and locked it.

"Sit down. Have a drink," he said.

Loka remembered the knife. He turned away without answering but kept Gyp in his field of vision. He'd faced knife fighters before. If this gypsy tried anything, he'd be ready for him.

Outside, Helmsley walked with Bolt for the short distance it took them to find cabs.

"I brought you into this because I needed . . . shall we say, your aid . . . in this arrangement," said Helmsley, twirling his tightly wrapped umbrella.

"Arrangement? You mean hijack," said Bolt.

Helmsley winced at the word. "Whatever you call it, I want no more violence. From here on, it is a legitimate business proposition."

"Legitimate?" laughed Bolt. "With a stolen hunk of sparklers?"

"Foreign art is often obtained through such channels as the tribesman, Loka. It is the way many rare objects have found their way into our leading museums and private collections."

"I wouldn't argue with you, laddy."

"Anything irregular from here on would only complicate matters—involve the police."

"The coppers are already onto this black. And what about the other guy with the dog, whoever he is?"

"Not our affair. After we sell the piece, Loka can be shipped out quietly, and that ends the matter." .

"Right," said Bolt, stepping into his cab. Later, as he neared the race track for his daily visit, he told himself, "Shipped out quietly—that's a nice way of putting it."

Diana was dreaming. A delightful dream. She was riding through a leafy glen with him. They were both on great white horses that seemed to float through the air. There were huge bright flowers and giant hummingbirds flickering in the dappled sunlight. He smiled and bent toward her. There was a persistent buzzing—no, a ringing. She woke up in the chair where she had dozed off. Her phone was ringing. Her room was dark. For a moment, she was in a panic, forgetting where she was, then wondering where the light switch was, or a lamp. The phone rang again, and she stumbled across the room, trying to reach it in the dark. She ran into the bed, fell across it, frantically found a lamp at the bedside table and snapped it on. The phone was on the other side of the bed. She slipped over and grasped it, put the receiver to her ear.

"Hello, hello?"

No one was there. Anxiously, she signaled the operator. It must have been him, trying to reach her from somewhere. From where? If she missed him now ... The operator's voice came in.

"Oh, Miss Palmer, we rang your room. The party is still on the line, leaving a message."

"Put him on, please!"

His voice came on, deep, reassuring. "Diana?"

"Oh, darling. I was asleep. I was afraid I missed your call. Are you all right? Where are you?"

"I'm fine. I'm calling from a phone booth in the park. Hyde Park. I've found a place here to hide Devil."

"Hide him? Why?"

"You haven't heard the news?"

"I was asleep. What happened?" she asked anxiously.

"Nothing I can tell you about now. I want you to do me a favor. Find a men's shop. There are some still open at this hour. Please buy me a tan trench coat and a cap, also a pair of green sunglasses. Dark ones."

"Why ..." she began.

"I'll explain later. Then wait in your room for my call."

"What size—the coat and hat?"

No reply for a moment. Then his voice. "I looked in my coat and hat. It says extra large on the coat. Cap is seven and three quarters."

"I have a back room on the first floor. Two windows. I'll leave a shade up, light on," said Diana. "Dear, did you lose your—no, you have them."

"They're looking for me. I need a change. I'll call back in an hour." Click.

She stared at the phone. She was lying across the bed on her stomach. In her rush to reach the phone, she'd knocked a lamp on the floor. "Looking for him? Why?" She hurriedly dressed, adjusted her makeup and went out to look for a man's shop. One tan trench coat, extra large; one cap, seven and three quarters. Dark green sunglasses. Why?

The butcher had taken off his apron and was about to call it a day when the tall man came in and bought six pounds of beef. "The missus and the kiddies are going to eat well tonight," he said cheerfully as he wrapped the order.

"Enjoy while you can, sir. The price of beef is going out of sight. Who can afford it anymore except the bloody millionaires?" The big man nodded, paid him and left without a words. The butcher wondered if he'd said something wrong. The big man didn't look like a millionaire.

The Phantom walked through the dark park with his package.

It amused him to think of the butcher's shock if he'd known the beef was going to be gobbled by a mountain wolf. The beef was costly, even though he had asked for an inexpensive cut. He knew nothing of dog foods. Devil required raw meat. The big animal was curled under thick bushes at the side of a lake. The Phantom dropped half the meat before him and watched as he attacked it. He placed the rest of the package behind a bench where it could not be seen. This was a good hideout for Devil. He was concealed on all sides, and had water that he could reach by barely moving his long head. When the wolf had finished his dinner, he was patted, told to stay—which he would do until doomsday if necessary. His master walked off. Lovers sat on the benches, a policeman strolled by. The park lamps were on, reflecting in the lake, and the lights of the city shone behind the dark trees.

Diana returned breathlessly to her room. She had found a store, made the purchases, and run all the way back. She raised a window, pulled up a shade and sat in the chair, waiting. Her name was whispered in the dark alley. She leaped to her feet as the big figure moved silently through the window into the room. She jumped into his arms. After their greeting was satisfactorily accomplished, she sat beside him as he told her the story of Loka and Duke. Also that the police were looking for him, but with the slight change of costume she had bought, they'd have no way of spotting him.

After putting on the new coat, cap and substituting green sunglasses for the brown ones he had worn, they went out to dinner without fear of detection and made plans for the following morning. Loka must be found before the police found him. They'd never believe his story about Duke's death. Worse, his identity as the brother of Bangalla's President Lamanda Luaga would be discovered by newspapers all over the world as well as by Luaga's enemies at home. Either Loka had gone off with friends (friends who didn't know his name?) or, more likely, had been found by mob- sters. Two leads, he told her. An art dealer named Helmsley —a vague lead at best, it seemed— and a gambler type who belched. Diana thought that was funny. She wanted to be the one who found him.

"Please let me help you. I feel so useless doing nothing. After all, Lamanda Luaga is a friend of mine, too."

"I'd rather have you useless and safe. There's a dangerous game going on here, Diana. Such high stakes always attract mobsters."

"Helmsley, the art dealer, doesn't sound like a mobster."

"Seems unlikely," he admitted. He pressed her hand. "Diana, there must be a wonderful matinée—opera, ballet, or play. Please keep out of this."

She smiled, ate her sherbet, and made no promises.

CHAPTER 11

It was a rare autumn day in London, sunny and dry. Nannies wheeled prams in the park. Oldsters sat on benches reading or enjoying the sun. The Phantom led Diana to Devil's hideout. The wolf had remained where he had been left. He greeted them happily but did not move, so perfect was his training.

"You wanted to help me. You can, now," he said. "I located a kennel on the outskirts 'of town near the race track. Take Devil out of the park, hail a taxi, put him in, and wait for me."

Her eyes sparkled. "You're going to the track to find the gambling belcher . . . or is it the belching gambler? Please let me go with you," she pleaded.

"No." There was a finality in his tone that ended further discussion. "Take in a matinée. If I don't find the belcher, which is most likely, I'll meet you at the hotel."

"And if you find him?"

"Then we will see." That was the end of that. She led Devil as he asked, and waited at the curb with a taxi. He joined her swiftly, a quick kiss, and he was gone. She returned to the park, sat on a bench and watched the swans.

He was right, of course, she told herself. She mustn't interfere. He was not playing games. This was serious business. But Diana was not your average girl-next-door. Olympic diving champion, pilot, explorer, now a UN medical administrator—a job that had taken her to many remote and often dangerous places. She was a daring girl and liked adventure. Otherwise, she would have remained a socialite in Westchester and would hardly be the sweetheart of a masked man who lived in a cave surrounded by pygmies. She wouldn't even be on this bench now, she told herself. She wouldn't get involved. But she wanted a taste of this adventure, a little harmless excitement.

She went to a phone booth, and after searching through "Antiques" and "Art Dealers" found a listing for the only familiar name in the business—Cunningham & Helmsley. As she strolled toward the nearby gallery, she told herself she didn't want to see actors in a stage play when this real-life drama was so close to her. She wanted to see one of the real-life actors, even if he had a minor, unimportant role. Helmsley.

Number 7 Savile Place was the discreet address of the most expensive hotel in London. It was small, luxurious, and discriminating. Its stupendous rates could be afforded by only the richest of American, German and Japanese industrialists; by superstars of film and rock; and by the new billionaires of the Middle East, the oil potentates. It was into the lavish suite of one of the latter that Helmsley was ushered. Two giant black guards, figures from feudal times, were in the foyer. They wore gold turbans, crimson silk shirts and baggy pants, and gleaming jeweled scimitars in their golden belts.

The Sheik of Suda-Kalara sat on a large pillow, puffing on a huge waterpipe ornamented with silver and jewels. The apparatus gurgled and bubbled as he drew on it. The Sheik was a lean man with piercing eyes under heavy brows. He wore a short trim black beard and was simply dressed in his desert outfit. His only adornment was a necklace of chunks of diamonds, emeralds, and rubies. Helmsley gasped when he saw it and, as he bowed before the seated ruler, made a quick estimate as to its value. Colossal! A shrewd older man wearing a turban and robe stood near the Sheik, obviously an advisor.

Helmsley had had some dealings with this Sheik before, selling him paintings and objets d'art, and knew him for a hard bargainer. As for Suda-Kalara, he knew only that it was one of the smallest and most backward of the Gulf kingdoms—with one of the largest reserves of oil. He launched into his sales talk immediately. One did not indulge in small talk with the Sheik. He produced a photo of the sacred image of the Llongo—one that he had taken himself during his visit to Bangalla—and told the story of the image, beginning with King Solomon and the Queen of Sheba.

That was a good beginning since the Sheik, like a dozen other Middle Eastern potentates, claimed the glamorous queen as an ancestor, a fact that Helmsley knew. It was for this reason that he had picked the Sheik for his first attempt. Strong family interest plus adequate cash—an unfailing combination. He had guessed correctly. The Sheik was fascinated. He studied the photo intently. His aide gave him a magnifying glass for a closer inspection. He was also fascinated by the legend of the-curse. It soon appeared that the Sheik knew about this object. He had read the newspaper stories about the valuable image that had once been the property of his illustrious ancestress.

Helmsley assured him as to its authenticity. He had personally obtained the object from the nephew of the Llongo High Chief. On this fact he pledged his honor as a reputable art dealer. The Sheik nodded. He knew Cunningham & Helmsley. He also knew how much ancient art reached the marketplace, stolen and smuggled from its place of origin. It was not the first time the Sheik had considered such art. He and his ilk were among the few who could afford such costly works.

As to price? Helmsley mentioned three million pounds sterling. The Sheik lifted his eyebrows and glanced at his aide, who threw up his hands in mock horror. The Sheik shook his head and offered a half million. Helmsley accepted the small cup of Turkish coffee offered by one of the giant blacks and shook his head. The Sheik bubbled and gurgled on his pipe and studied the photo. It was obvious that he was itching to own this ancient masterpiece.

"One million," he said.

"His Highness's final offer," said the aide sternly.

Helmsley shook his head. This would be giving it away. It went back and forth like this, bubbling, gurgling, sipping, until they agreed on a figure: one million eight hundred thousand British pounds sterling (roughly four and a half million American dollars).

Helmsley stood up, dizzy with success. He could hardly believe it had happened so fast. Sizable deals sometimes took weeks or months. This, the biggest deal of his life, had taken a half hour.

"This will be a cash transaction, naturally, your Highness."

"Naturally," said the aide as the Sheik nodded. "If after examination, there is any evidence of misrepresentation, the money will be returned," he added, his smile fading, his eyes cold.

"That goes without saying."

"In such an unlikely event, his Highness has the means to recover the money, no matter where it will have wandered."

Helmsley glanced at the immobile giant guards, at the Sheik who sat impassively gurgling and bubbling on his water-pipe.

"You need have no fear. The object is genuine," said Helmsley. The gurgling and bubbling stopped. Helmsley settled back to the floor when the Sheik spoke.

"The image must be here, in my possession within two hours. At that time, we depart for my country."

"Two hours?"

"Two hours, precisely, or his Highness cannot purchase the object, Mr. Helmsley," said the aide.

"All right, I'll do it, I'll be back," he said, racing for the door. He caught himself, bowed to the seated ruler, then ran out. Sheik and aide smiled at each other. The ruler stared at the photo admiringly.

"From the Queen herself, it has returned. This will be the jewel of my crown."

Helmsley was too rushed to wait for the stately, slow-moving elevator. He ran down the stairs three at a time. The sedate desk clerk lifted his eyebrows as the man dashed out. People did not dash at 7 Savile Place. There were no taxis in sight. He thought rapidly. A half hour to Bolt's house, a half hour back. No, something he must do first. There might be some difficulty in that game room. His office was only a short distance. He started toward it, half running, clutching his bowler and umbrella, an impeccable Londoner. In the back of his top desk drawer was a small pearl-handled revolver. Both he and his partner Cunningham kept such a weapon handy. Their showroom was filled with costly objects. There had been no robbery attempts yet, but you never knew. Now he might need the gun. He hoped not. He abhorred violence. Feared it. But one million eight hundred thousand was one million eight hundred thousand.

"Mr. Helmsley is not in. Can Mr. Cunningham help you?" said the woman behind the open glass panel. Diana stood in the foyer of the gallery.

"When will Mr. Helmsley be in?"

"Hard to say," said the woman with a shadow of a grin. "He might be in any minute or—who knows?"

A man appeared behind the woman. "She's here to see Mr. Helmsley," she said, turning to him. He looked at Diana through the glass. Simply but expensively dressed, the fresh look of a young lady, not like what he often contemptuously referred to as "one of Helmsley's bawds."

"I'm Mr. Cunningham. Did you wish to see Mr. Helmsley personally"—he stressed that word lightly—"or may I help you?"

Diana thought quickly. She couldn't pretend to be one of his friends, in case he walked in suddenly.

"Thank you. That would be very kind," she said.

Mr. Cunningham smiled and disappeared, the door clicked open and he was waiting for her in the showroom.

"Anything particular in mind, or would you prefer to browse," he said.

"Thanks. I'm fond of primitive pieces, pre-Columbian, African, Oriental."

"This way please." She followed him as he pointed out and explained a variety of small statues and artifacts.

"Do you know Helmsley?"

"No, not at all. Er, a mutual friend recommended the gallery."

"Perhaps someone I might know?" He was only being polite.

"Perhaps. A Mr. Walker." She had to smile when she said it. "Will Mr. Helmsley be back soon?"

"Back? He hasn't been-in yet today. Leads odd hours, though he manages to make the race track by the opening gun." He smiled apologetically, as though he had said too much.

"Oh, he likes racing? I didn't know," said Diana, glad to find some safe aspect of the missing man to talk about. What am I doing here, she asked herself, talking about a man I don't know and care less about. Oh, it's fun. Carry on, she told herself.

"Like the horses? He's an addict. Out there every day he can get away from here—and sometimes when he can't," said Mr. Cunningham, allowing himself a little joke. But there was a bitter edge to it. Helmsley's habit was obviously a matter of contention between them.

"Is your Mr. Walker also a racing fan?" he went on, probing politely for the connection.

"Oh no," she laughed. "I believe they knew each other in Bangalla." The word seemed to have a peculiar effect on the white-haired man, and she regretted saying it. But why? After all, it was a big place. Many tourists.

"Oh, do you know Bangalla?" he said.

"In a way. I've been there. Oh, this is an interesting piece. What is it?" she said, changing the subject. He was about to answer when Helmsley walked in.

He walked rapidly to his desk in a far corner, took something from it and was heading back to the door when Cunningham called to him. "Oh, Mr. Helmsley, a moment please."

"I'm in a terrible hurry. Appointment," he said, coming toward them reluctantly.

"This is Miss ... ?"

"Palmer," said Diana.

"Miss Palmer had asked for you, Helmsley. She was sent here by a mutual friend, a Mr. Walker—correct?—of Bangalla." He pronounced the last word softly. Helmsley's impatience vanished. He looked sharply at her.

"Walker? Who is he?"

"A man, an official in Mawitaan," she said slowly. "He said to see your gallery when I came here. That's all."

"Are you from Mawitaan?"

"No, New York."

Helmsley glanced quickly at his pocket watch. "I must leave. Would you care to walk downstairs with me? I'd like to hear more about Walker."

"Are you coming back?" said Cunningham. "We've a busy day, you know."

"I'll try."

"The horses can live without you for a day," said Cunningham awkwardly, trying to make a joke that didn't ring true. Helmsley laughed without humor and nodded.

"No horses today. Shall we go?"

Why not? thought Diana. "Thank you, Mr. Cunningham. I'd like to come back and see more of your things."

"Please, any time, Miss Palmer."

As they walked down the stairs, Helmsley questioned her quickly. He seemed in a terrible hurry. Who was Walker? What did he do?

"He's a peace officer" (Keeper of the Peace) ". . . a sort of guardian" (Guardian of the Eastern Dark). Diana could hardly keep from laughing. This was such fun, playing a game with this dapper little man with his waxed mustache, bowler, umbrella, such a proper Englishman.

"Peace officer, guardian, can't seem to recall . . said Helmsley, perplexed. "Is he there now?"

"No, I believe not."

"Where?"

"Here."

"Here in London?"

She nodded. He stopped on the sidewalk and looked at her. Since his return from Bangalla two years before, he had never met anyone who'd been there. Hardly anyone had even heard of the backward little country. It was one of those nations that had suddenly evolved on the edge of the jungle. Now, here was a woman, and a man, both with connections in Bangalla. Today. A thought popped into his mind.

"Does he have a big dog?"

Diana was caught by surprise. "Yes," she said.

"I'm trying to place him. Did he bring the dog with him?" Diana nodded, suddenly confused. Odd questions.

"Have you heard of the Llongo?"

She nodded again. "Yes, a tribe in Bangalla."

He looked at her without expression. "Not many people could answer that," he said.

"Really?" she said. What's he getting at? she wondered.

A cab stopped at the curb in response to his hand signal. He took her arm firmly.

"Come along," he said. "I want to hear more about Mr. Walker." She drew back, surprised.

"No, of course not. I—I'm busy."

The cab driver watched cynically as Helmsley whispered in her ear. Reluctant young women were not new to him. But Helmsley was not whispering romance.

"I have a gun in my pocket. It's pointed at your stomach. Get in, or I'll shoot. I mean it."

His face was grim, his eyes desperate. She knew he meant it. Had he gone mad? She got into the cab. He kept hold of her arm and called an address to the driver, then closed the panel that separated him from the back seat.

"What are you trying to do?" said Diana. That's all she could think of to say.

"It's no accident that you came to our gallery today. "Did Mr. Walker, this man with the big gray dog, send you?"

How did he know Devil was big and gray? "No, it was my own idea."

"Why?"

"I like art, primitives."

"That's a lie."

"Mr. Helmsley, I don't know what this is all about. Or what you're up to. If you don't stop this cab and let me out, I'll start screaming."

"Oh, don't do that," he said, glancing at the driver through the glass panel. The man was busy looking ahead at traffic. Helmsley swung, hitting her sharply on the jaw. She fell back. He put her head on his shoulder, his arm about her, and put his lips against her cheek. The driver glanced at his rear view mirror and saw what looked like lovebirds. He grinned. The bloke was a fast worker.

When they reached their destination, a small house in Soho, Diana was beginning to groan and move her head. Helmsley hurriedly thrust money into the driver's hand, then half-lifted, half-dragged her out of the cab. The driver looked on in alarm.

"Is she sick? Can I help, sir?" he asked.

"Nothing. She's just, you know, expecting."

The driver grinned and watched until the man had carried his burden into a basement door. The man knocked on the door, it was opened, and he went inside. The cab went on. You get all kinds.

In the game room, Gyp and Loka stared at the girl.

"Who the hell is that?" demanded Gyp.

"Why you bring her here?" said Loka.

"Bolt'll murder you," said Gyp.

Helmsley shook his head impatiently as he carried Diana to an armchair. "I'll explain. This is important. It's about the other man."

"What other man?"

"The man with the dog."

The Phantom left Devil at a boarding kennel on the highway. He saw to it that the big animal had roomy quarters with a large open run. For food, only raw meat. Yes, horse meat would do. For how long? A day or two. What kind of dog is that, mister? Looks like a wolf. Doesn't it, though?

Even though he had changed his outer clothing, he was taking no chances on being picked up by the police for questioning. He had an uneasy feeling that time was extremely short. He drove on to the nearby race track, the one closest to town. Searching for a gambler at a race track, among twenty thousand gamblers? One who belched? Ten percent, or two thousand, might be similarly afflicted. But he'd worked on slimmer leads, against greater odds.

He went into the stands, and began talking to the touts, the men giving out tips for-a fee. They'd know all the regulars. A race was on. The crowd was roaring.

"Big man. Wears a black bowler. Diamond pin in his tie. Red face. Fancy dresser. Belches a lot."

He got a lot of odd glances from the busy touts, and no answers. "What do you want him for?"

"He owes me some money."

"Nope, can't help you."

"Belches? How do you mean?"

"Like this—burrrrp."

"Nope, can't help you."

"My cousin belches, drinks beer all day. That's him over there." A short fat man, in a sweatshirt, a beer bottle tilted to his lips. "No, that's not the one."

"Well, he belches."

"Thanks."

It went on like that, for an hour or two. He asked the clerks at the pari-mutuel windows, the men's room attendants, the bartenders, the concessionaires who sold fish and chips. "What's his name?"

"I forgot it."

"Forgot? And he owes you money? Man!" Another race, more questions, no answers. It was late afternoon now. One more race. It began to look hopeless. But like the horse that had won the last one, it was a long shot. Twenty-to-one? More like a hundred- to-one. But long shots come in, now and then.

A deep voice rumbled behind him.

"You looking for somebody?" (Burp.)

The Phantom turned, and faced Bolt. The clerk's description had been a good one. Florid complexion, cigar in his teeth, black derby, and diamond stickpin, loud shirt and suit. Also a firm jaw and hard eyes.

"Yes, I am. It might be you."

"I don't owe you any money. Never saw you before." (Burp.)

"True. But we have a mutual friend."

"Yeah? Who?"

"Loka."

A young man wearing a cap and a dark turtleneck jersey under a topcoat had been standing idly at the side, seeming to pay no attention. Bolt glanced at him and he was behind the Phantom in one step. The Phantom felt a hard object pressed against his spine. A familiar object. The barrel of a gun. The crowd was roaring as the horses came into the stretch.

"He's got a silencer. If he shoots, no one could hear," said Bolt.

"Not necessary. I've got a big deal—for you and Loka,"

"What deal?" (Burp.)

"Can't talk here. I have to talk with you and Loka, but I must be sure you have the image."

Bolt clamped down on his cigar at that.

"You know about that?" The Phantom nodded. Bolt studied him. "You that other guy, the guy with the dog?" The Phantom nodded, "So Loka was lying, said he didn't know you."

"No, he didn't lie. He doesn't know me." "

"Who are you?"

"Can't talk here."

Bolt nodded and walked at his side toward the exit. The man with the gun followed closely. Outside, they reached a large car with curtained windows. The Phantom was waved to the front seat next to the driver—the man with the gun. Bolt sat in back, a gun in his hand.

"Ready to talk now?"

"Not until we get there."

"Get where?"

"Where Loka is, and the image."

Bolt's voice rumbled. He laughed. "Okay, laddy, you better have good answers." They drove on in silence.

CHAPTER 12

Diana was aware of men's voices arguing. One was sharp, cockney. Another foreign, musical. The third, well-bred English—Helmsley! She opened her eyes with a start. They didn't notice her at first. They were yelling at each other. Something glittered near her. It came into focus. The sacred image. She'd seen a black-and-white newsprint photo of it.

The reality was startling. Vivid, shining, brilliant gold, reds, greens, shimmering whites, almost blinding.

"She's come to," said Gyp. He was a swarthy little man, with greasy, slicked-back hair. "Talk to her. Ask her who the guy is. The guy with the dog."

"I've no time for that. I tell you I've got to go," said Helmsley.

"Not until Bolt gets back. You heard him," said Gyp.

"You do not go without me," said the black man.

That must be Loka, nephew of the High Chief, Lamanda's brother. She recognized the eminent brother in this weaker face. They were arguing, but not about her. She felt her jaw, and the scene in the cab came back to her. Helmsley had hit her. He didn't seem the sort who was capable of that. You never could tell about men.

"I'm wasting time. I tell you I've got to be back in an hour or the deal's off," said Helmsley.

"Bolt said wait here," said Gyp. "You wait."

"I think you lie. You want to steal image," said Loka.

Helmsley stamped his foot in exasperation.

"I tell you, the deal is made. One million eight hundred thousand quid. If I get back by three!" he shouted.

"Oh sure," said Gyp. "What you been smoking, man?"

"For such an amount, why would anyone be in that big a hurry?" said Loka sarcastically.

Helmsley took a card from his pocket and waved it angrily. "Here it is, in black and white. The Sheik of Suda-Kalara. Seven Savile Place. Waiting to give us, give me one million eight hundred thousand British pounds sterling cash for that object—if I get it there by three," he shouted.

"You said that before," said Gyp calmly. "Bolt will be back by five. You can wait."

"Lady," said Loka. "Who is the man with the dog?"

"His name is Walker. Nobody anybody ever heard of," shouted Helmsley, reaching the end of his patience.

"Did he see you kill that Duke?" said Gyp.

"I never heard of no man called Walker," said Loka. "Why do the police want him, lady?"

"I don't know," she said, her head spinning.

"You better know when Bolt gets here. He likes answers, lady," said Gyp, pronouncing the last word sarcastically.

"What is your part in this, lady?" said Loka.

She looked at him steadily, suddenly angry with him for what he was and what he had done.

"I am a friend of Lamanda Luaga," she said, staring into his bloodshot eyes. He reacted as though he had been hit with a whip. He recoiled, his body trembled, he threw up his hands as though avoiding a blow.

"Who?" said Gyp.

Loka shook his head and turned away, too upset to talk. She had touched a vital, tender spot.

"Never mind her. Our time's running out. Gyp, I've got to meet that man in an hour—fifty minutes now!"

"Bolt said wait."

"Come with me. You can see for yourself the deal is good."

"The deal can wait!"

Helmsley saw in Gyp one of those exasperating toadies who, once programmed, could not be diverted. Like a robot.

"You stupid Gypsy!" he shouted and rushed to the image, taking it under one arm. Gyp moved two steps before the door and drew his long knife.

"Loka, stop him," he shouted. As Loka turned, Helmsley flashed his pearl-handled gun.

"Get away from that door, Gyp," he commanded.

"Don't touch that! Put it down!" screamed Loka, hysterical when he saw the image under Helmsley's arm, He started toward him. Helmsley pointed the gun at him.

"Stay where you are or I'll blow your head off," he said. Loka backed away, staring, frantic, sweat pouring from his face. Helmsley took a step toward the door. Gyp was crouched, the knife in his hand, his eyes like slits.

"You haven't got the guts to use that, you upper-class pig," he snarled, then moved slowly toward the dealer. Diana stared, frozen by the violence and hate.

"Put that gun down, before I slit your throat," said Gyp in the, same low, deadly voice, moving ever so slowly forward.

The gun exploded like a cannon in the low-ceilinged room. Gyp had a surprised look on his face as he dropped the knife, clutched his stomach, and fell to the floor.

"No man, wait," said Loka. "You can't take. You can't touch. The curse!"

"I have touched it—no curse," said Helmsley hoarsely. "Don't move."

"Let me go with you," pleaded Loka. "I can help. Don't leave me. They will kill me."

"I don't need you. Stay where you are," said Helmsley in the same hoarse tones. As he slowly backed toward the door, he looked at Diana, who stared at him, terrified, and amazed that so much brutality was in this innocuous-looking proper Englishman.

As he backed up, a hand grasped his ankle. It was Gyp, lying on the floor. The sudden touch startled Helmsley, whose nerves were at the breaking point. He whirled about, but the grip clung, tripping him. He fell forward, hitting the floor, the image under him. He uttered a shriek, an agonized wrenching sound. Diana shuddered. She had once heard wounded buffalo shriek like that—almost a bellow.

Still shrieking, he got to his knees and half-turned toward Diana and Loka. His hands clutched the image. The horns were driven deep into his chest. He was suddenly silent, staring at the image, at his chest, at the blood. His face drained white. Diana and Loka watched, transfixed. He opened his mouth, trying to talk, but only a noise came out. Then he collapsed limply, his head falling back. The body settled. No more movement. Diana covered her eyes. She was shaking with the horror of the scene.

Loka walked slowly to the bar, poured himself a large whiskey and gulped it down, then bent over Helmsley. The man was dead. He tugged the horns free, then stood up with the image. There was blood on it. He took a bar towel and carefully wiped it clean. A thought suddenly came to him. That card. He went through the coat pockets and found it. He walked to Diana and shook her shoulder. The terrified girl uncovered her face. She looked up at him fearfully.

"I do not read good. Read it to me," he said. He was breathing hard, and sweat rolled from him. Diana stared at the card that swam before her eyes.

"Read it," he shouted, almost hysterical again.

She clenched her fists and focused on the words written in ink.

"Sheik of Suda-Kalara. Seven Savile Place," she read.

He murmured the words half aloud, to fix them in his memory, then dropped the card on the floor and ran to the door. He paused while he wrapped the towel around the image.

"You are friend of my brother. I will not hurt you." He opened the door and had another thought. "If you were not friend of my brother, I would not hurt you. I do not hurt ladies." And he slammed the door.

Diana jumped to her feet. Gyp was on the floor, staring at her, his eyes pleading for help. Helmsley was curled up near him. Someone called Bolt was coming. Avoiding the clutching hands of Gyp, she rushed to the door and slammed it behind her, running into the open air, fleeing this house of horrors.

Her mind was racing. Call the police? Go back to the hotel and wait? She saw Loka jumping into a cab a half block away. He had the image. Anger replaced her fear. The Phantom was risking his life to find that image. So close, yet so far now, as the cab sped off. She must follow, not let him get away. She hailed a cab and followed.

"Seven Savile Place," she told the driver.

As her mind cleared in the cab, the scene she had just witnessed fell into place. One man wounded. Fatally? One man dead, accidentally. Accidentally? The swarthy man had tripped him, but the image had killed him. The curse? She shivered. The Sheik, whoever that was, must be told. Anyone could afford that fortune for an art object must be one of high rank, position, prestige—like her friends at the UN.

He would not want to be associated with the crimes involved in this affair. He would flee from it like the plague. He would thank her. He would call the police, she told herself.

The cab reached the address. She recognized it, an exclusive place where she had once attended a most elegant tea. Then she reached for her purse. It wasn't there. She panicked. She must have lost it during the cab ride with Helmsley or in that house. She couldn't go back there.

"I forgot my purse. I'll send money down from upstairs. Will you wait, please," she said as the doorman opened the cab door. He heard her.

"Are you a guest here, Miss? I can advance the fare," he said.

"I—I am a guest of the Sheik of Suda-Kalara," she said quickly, thinking, he'd be glad to pay this fare when I tell him what I know.

"Oh yes," said the doorman, grinning knowingly. "I'll take care of it, Miss."

As she entered the lobby, she wondered about that knowing grin. Perhaps the Sheik had many "ladies" visiting him. She smiled. Did she look like one of those? At the front desk, she gave her name to the supercilious clerk who was adjusting the white carnation in his lapel. "Mention the name Loka —L-O-K-A," she added. He raised an eyebrow and gave her the same knowing grin as he took the phone to call the suite. He turned from her as he spoke, so she could hear nothing but the last words. "Very good," he said.

"They request that you wait for a few moments, Miss Palmer," he said, smirking. "There is a lounge through that arch." She nodded and followed directions. She hoped there was a ladies' room. There was. And a kindly old white-haired attendant. Diana stared into the mirror. Her hair and the little makeup she used were a mess. And that jaw! No wonder the grins and smirks. She had no comb, no makeup. But the kindly attendant, an angel in disguise, lent her comb and lipstick after she had washed her face. Her jaw showed a slight swelling. It was tender to the touch. It could have been worse. It might have been broken, teeth loosened. But everything was in place. Poor Helmsley was a slight, if desperate, man.

She thanked the old lady, apologized for lack of a tip and returned to the lounge proper where she sank gratefully into a deep sofa. What was Kit doing? Had he found his belcher? It might be a good idea to leave a message at her hotel, telling where she was in case he tried to reach her. There was a phone at her side, a hotel extension. As she reached for it, the phone rang. She looked about. No one was in sight. She picked up the receiver.

"Miss Palmer?" It was the condescending voice of the desk clerk.

"Yes?"

"They will see you now. At once," he said. It was an order. No time for a call now. Later. She walked quickly to the elevator, going over in her mind what she would tell the Sheik. If Loka was already there, all the better.

Loka was already there. He had been received by the same supercilious clerk who looked askance at this roughly dressed black man clutching some ungainly object wrapped in a dirty towel. The doorman had entered with him and stood just behind him in case of trouble.

"I am here to see the Sheik," he said, forgetting the rest of it. The clerk looked at him stonily. "Deliveries are made at the service entrance," he said coldly. Loka's nerves were already frayed. He didn't need this arrogant white to put him down.

"I am no servant The Sheik awaits this. Kindly announce," he said firmly. "Say, the object from Mr. Helmsley is here."

The clerk shrugged. Seven Savile was accustomed to rich eccentrics. He phoned and was told to send the man up. He waved Loka to the elevator, then exchanged a look of disgust with the doorman. All sorts were coming here these days. Clutching the towel-wrapped object to his chest like a baby, he was ushered into the drawing room of the suite by one of the giant black guards. The Sheik Was no longer on the floor with his waterpipe. He was seated at a Sheraton desk closing a briefcase. He looked at Loka in surprise.

"Where is Mr. Helmsley?"

"He sent me, sir."

"Highness," corrected the aide, watching with a puzzled look.

"Highness," said Loka, bowing.

"Is that the image?" said the Sheik. Loka nodded. "Let me see it."

"You must give me one million eight hundred thousand British pounds sterling," said Loka carefully, making sure to get it right.

The Sheik looked at him with annoyance. "Let me see it," he repeated sharply. One of the giant blacks started toward Loka. Loka nodded, quickly moved to the coffee table, unwrapped the towel, and placed the glittering image on the glass surface. All the others, the Sheik, his aide and the two giant blacks, showed amazement, at the stunning sight, each in his own way.

The Sheik moved toward it, hands extended, like a child reaching for a bright new toy.

"No," said Loka sharply. "Do not touch it."

The Sheik turned on him angrily.

"The curse," he said quickly. "If one not of Llongo, touches it, he dies."

"He dies?" repeated the aide named Taras.

"It kills him," said Loka. "Believe my words. I have seen it happen, thrice!"

The Sheik looked at the image intently, then at Loka.

"You are of Llongo?"

"I am."

"Your name?"

"Loka."

The Sheik looked at his aide, who nodded.

"Nephew of the High Chief. He stole it," said Taras.

Loka reacted angrily. "I did not steal. I am Llongo. It is mine, as much as any other's."

"We understand," said the Sheik, smiling. He seemed not

displeased. To the contrary. This was the guarantee of authenticity.

"And where is Mr. Helmsley?" said the aide.

"He sent me," said Loka shortly.

"That was not the question," said the aide sharply.

Loka considered a moment. Where would Helmsley be? He recalled the endless discussion between Helmsley and Bolt.

"He went to the track. Race horse."

The Sheik looked incredulously at Taras.

"At this time, with such money awaiting him, he would go to the track?" said the Sheik.

"He sent me," said Loka firmly. "I am to bring him the money. One million eight hundred thousand pounds British sterling. Cash," he added. The Sheik smiled at this childlike recitation.

Taras picked up the towel and held it before the Sheik.

"That's blood," he said, pointing to the damp, reddish- brown stains. The Sheik's smile was gone. The black giants looked on impassively, understanding not a word.

"Where is Mr. Helmsley?" said the aide sternly. "Did you kill him?"

"Kill him?" said Loka with genuine anguish. "No, never."

The Sheik said something to the aide in their language.

Taras nodded.

"We have no time to pursue this matter thoroughly. It is important that we know if Helmsley is alive or dead."

"I ... I ... alive. Why should he be dead?" said Loka anxiously.

"Who else knows about this image? His partner Mr. Cunningham?"

"No, not him."

"Are you certain?"

"Certain."

The phone rang. Taras answered, muttered something to the Sheik, who shook his head. The aide looked at Loka.

"Do you know a woman named Palmer?" he said.

Loka looked bewildered. "Palmer? No. Never," he said.

"She said to mention your name."

"Me?" His eyes widened. The picture came to him of the girl, dazed and terrified, sitting in the chair. "It might be her."

"Her?" said the aide sharply.

"She. . . she knows about the image," he said weakly.

Taras talked into the phone and hung up.

"Who is she? Quickly, man."

"I don't know, I don't know," said Loka honestly, confused by this complicated web that tightened with every move. "I never saw her before an hour ago. She knows the man with the dog."

CHAPTER 13

The soft sound of the bell and the entrance of the girl interrupted the questioning of Loka. Diana looked with amazement at the two giant black guards who bowed solemnly and escorted her in. The men and their costumes had to be out of an old operetta. In the long drawing room, a man in a flowing blue burnoose bowed his head slightly. Loka, looking terrified, stood rigidly near the glittering image on the coffee table. But the man seated on the sofa, clad in a creamy white robe and a dazzling necklace of enormous jewels, had to be the Sheik. His lean handsome face was without expression as his glance traveled from her head to her feet and back up again. He glanced at the man in blue, who spoke.

"Yes?" was all he said.

"Your Highness, I must tell you about that object," she said, gesturing at the image.

"Do not listen. She will lie," said Loka anxiously.

The Sheik looked at him coldly. The glance was like a whiplash. Then he looked toward the man in blue.

"We are about to depart. State your business quickly," said the man in blue.

"I am here because it's my understanding you are about to buy, or have bought, that image," she said.

"Continue," said Taras.

"I must know. If you are not buying it, there's no point to my continuing," she said, not knowing if the Sheik understood a word she was saying. He understood.

"Do as you are told. Continue," he said, in the flat quiet tone of a man whose words have always been obeyed.

"To begin with," she went on nervously, disconcerted by the complete lack of expression on his face (as if he were made of wax, she told herself), "that image was stolen from the Llongo tribe by this and another man." If she expected that announcement to create a sensation, she was wrong. No change of expression from either man. "Do you understand what I said? Am I making myself clear?" No expression. The Sheik made a slight movement. He looked at his gold wristwatch. "One of the men involved, an old guide, was killed before they left Bangalla."

"The image killed him," Loka blurted out.

The Sheik barely glanced at him, then back to Diana. The man in blue watched her intently. Didn't death matter to these men?

"The man called Duke who came here with Loka and the image was also killed, twenty-four hours ago, here in London."

"The image . . ." began Loka. A look from the man in blue silenced him.

"Do you know the art dealer Helmsley?" she went on. That struck something. They both looked at her sharply. The man in blue nodded ever so slightly.

"A half hour ago—a half hour ago," she began. Her voice became choked. The scene was still vivid in her mind. She got hold of herself and went on. "About a half hour ago, Helmsley was killed."

That woke them up. The Sheik glared at Loka and uttered a harsh foreign word. The man in blue spoke through clenched teeth.

"You lied. You told us he was alive." His voice was cold and angry, a frightening combination. Loka clasped his hands together in anguish, sweating profusely, his eyes rolling.

"She's lying. She's lying," he began.

"I can take you there. I'm sure he hasn't been moved," said Diana, feeling sorry for the wretched man. The man in blue glanced at one of the big guards and muttered something. The guard moved to Loka, towering a full head over him, and held his arm.

"You will tell the truth, completely, Loka," the man in blue said coolly. "Or he will break your back." He muttered another word and the giant put a hand on Loka's neck and applied pressure. Loka bent and screamed. Diana shuddered. This wasn't what she wanted. She wanted police.

"He's dead . . . dead. I didn't do it . . . ask her . . . she saw," said Loka, his voice cracking under the pain.

The man in blue muttered again and the giant released Loka,

who straightened up painfully. Then they looked at Diana. She nodded and told them exactly what happened . . . Helmsley and the gun, Gyp and the knife, the fall on the image, the death. The Sheik and Taras stared at the image.

"It was that way?" asked Taras quietly.

"Exactly," said Diana.

The two continued to stare. They were no longer looking at a precious object. They were looking at a legend, looking with awe at the legend of the curse. These were not modern Western then. In their feudal fifteenth-century world, they lived with djinns and demons. They knew about the power of a curse. The Sheik did not conceal his excitement. He was not only acquiring a fabulous treasure. He was acquiring . . . magic! He muttered to his aide, and contemplated the image through half-lowered eyelids. Then he arose and left the room without a word.

"Miss Palmer," said Taras, suddenly polite, "who else knows of this offer of sale to his Highness?"

An odd question. She thought for a moment.

"Only Loka and I—yes, and the wounded Gypsy."

"Loka spoke of a man with a dog. A friend of yours?"

"He is a law enforcer from Bangalla."

"He searches for the image?"

"Yes, and for Loka."

"Who . . . who is he?" asked Loka desperately. "Jungle Patrol?" Loka would never know that he had made a lucky guess. The Phantom was the unknown commander of the Patrol, but he was not conducting this mission for them. Diana did not answer him.

"And does he know of this offer to us, and the subsequent events, the death of Helmsley, et cetera, et cetera?" Taras asked.

"He does not know about Helmsley or that Loka came here. Not yet. I intend to call him as soon as I have a moment."

"A good idea. You know where this law enforcer is?"

"Mr. Walker," said Diana.

"Where Mr. Walker can be reached?" he said, his voice kind.

"Not now. I'll leave a message at my hotel for him that I am here," she said.

"This Mr. Walker, he is someone special to you?" he said, smiling in a friendly way.

"He is my good friend."

"Ah yes. Then he will be concerned about your safety. He is a man to be envied," he added gallantly.

She nodded and smiled. The world was getting back to normal again. "May I use your phone now, please."

"In a moment," he smiled. "His Highness is busy with it now." He walked toward the door where the Sheik had exited.

"Will you excuse me for a moment. Please be seated," he said, gesturing to the sofa. "You also, Loka," he added.

Diana went to the sofa. Loka sat on an ottoman near the window. They sat in silence. She avoided his eyes.

"My brother," he began. She glanced at him, then looked away. He was quiet for a moment, drumming up courage. "Please," he said hesitantly, "if you see my brother . . . if you see Lamanda, will you kindly, please, not tell him about this."

She looked at him and felt a wave of sympathy. His voice had been anxious, sincere. He was wanted for three murders—for which he might have difficulty proving his innocence—and he was wanted for a robbery that made him an outcast among his people. Yet, his main concern, at least now, was that his brother should not know. She shook her head.

"He will not need me to tell him," she said.

He lowered his head in his hands. They sat in silence, watched by one of the big guards. The other one had gone out a side door. He reappeared carrying a tray with a brass pot and small brass cups containing thick sweet Turkish coffee. Diana accepted a cup gratefully. She needed something. The giant tapped Loka on the shoulder. He looked up, shook his head, and covered his face with his hands again. The aide Taras returned.

"You wish coffee, Loka?" he said. Loka shook his head. Taras shrugged and the guard left the room. Diana sipped her coffee. It tasted good. She realized she was hungry and wondered if there were any cookies.

"May I call my hotel now?" she asked.

"In a moment," he said. "We wish to thank you for your information. It has clarified many questions we had in this matter, and has enabled us to reach a satisfactory decision."

Loka looked up. "You will give me the money, one million eight hundred thousand British pounds sterling, cash?" he said.

"We will discuss that in a moment. Miss Palmer, are you living here in London?"

"No, New York."

"Ah yes. I should have known. Your accent. But you have relatives and friends here?" he continued, making conversation.

"Not really. Just my good friend," she said, smiling.

"Ah, the man with the dog. Mr. Walker?"

Diana tittered. She was feeling lightheaded. "Everybody thinks it's a dog. It's really a wolf."

Loka looked up at that. The word "wolf" rang a bell somewhere, but he couldn't place it.

"How unusual," said the polite man in the flowing blue burnoose.

"He's an unusual man," she said thickly. Her eyes were heavy. She suddenly realized how tired she was. It had been a dreadful day. She yawned and struggled to keep her eyes open. The room was spinning. The man in blue seemed to float before her and his voice came from a distance.

"You look tired, Miss Palmer. Close your eyes and rest."

"Do you mind . . . do you mind?" she tried to say, but the words wouldn't come out right. Her tongue felt heavy, her eyes felt heavy, he said something else but he was too far away.

The cup fell from her hand, spilling a little coffee on her skirt. She toppled sideways onto the couch, her head hanging over the edge. At a signal, a guard came and straightened her out to a prone position. Loka watched in alarm. He was familiar with knockout drops. The coffee! He looked anxiously at the aide. The Sheik walked in. Over his creamy burnoose he wore a magnificent scarlet robe trimmed in gold braid. Instead of a hood, he now wore a golden turban, set off by an enormous ruby that twinkled like a headlight.

For the moment, Loka forgot the image. His mind was on the drugged girl who was a friend of his brother.

"She is a lady—high-class type—you must not hurt her," he said awkwardly.

"She is going with us. You are going with us," said Taras.

"With you? You must pay me. I will not go with you. Pay me. Pay me one million eight—"

The black giant approached him and took his arm.

"I need you," said the Sheik. "I respect the legend of your people. In my palace, none will be permitted to touch the sacred image, none but you. You will guard it day and night." He said all this slowly, in measured tones, as though reading an official paper.

"Guard it night and day? Where?" said Loka, confused.

"In my palace," said the aide.

The Sheik walked to the door, having finished his conversation. Loka started after him. The guard took his arm and held him.

"I will not go. You cannot take the image. It is mine. Mine!" he shouted.

The Sheik turned at the door and glanced at the guard. The guard struck Loka across the cheek, a hard blow that shook him.

"You will learn to speak when you are spoken to," said Taras. "Not before."

The Sheik looked at the image. "The image was stolen from my family—from our Queen. It now returns to its rightful place—to me," he said.

"You promised to pay," said Loka frantically.

He was cuffed hard again.

"Pay for what is mine? Now silence, slave, or you will lose your tongue," said the Sheik in a matter-of-fact voice. He walked into the corridor, followed by a guard.

"Slave?" said Loka, gasping for breath.

Taras nodded. "We are an ancient kingdom. We hold to the old ways. You are now the property of his Highness."

"Property?" said Loka. "Property."

The aide ignored the question. A guard was pushing a wheelchair into the room. Diana was lifted from the couch. A black gown was slipped over her body, and she was placed in the wheelchair. A heavy veil was put over her head. She was completely covered. The guard wheeled her to the door. Through a side door, Loka saw a half-dozen bellboys carrying luggage into the corridor. Then he stared at the departing wheelchair.

"It was decided this way. We could not leave the girl to pass on information. That would be stupid, would it not, slave?"

The guard led him toward the door. Loka pulled back. "If you make trouble, he will break your back. We will say you were a robber—how do they say—a mugger." He pronounced it "muggaire."

Taras left the drawing room for a moment, then returned with a leather suitcase. He held it near the image. He nodded to Loka.

"Place it in there," he said.

Loka did as he was told. He locked the case.

"You will carry it now. You will always carry it, guard it, care for it, as his Highness commanded," said the aide as they walked to the door.

"How . . . how long?" said Loka, dazed, his mind reeling.

"Always means as long as you live. If you are a good slave, that will be a long time."

The guard gripped his arm tightly. He clutched the case.

They left the suite and descended in a special back elevator used by royalty and other important guests.

"Always. As long as you live."

CHAPTER 14

Bolt knocked sharply on the door, three times. The Phantom stood near him, and just behind was the young man with the gun partially concealed in his coat. The gunman had not spoken during the ride. But he balanced this by chewing loudly and juicily on gum. The Phantom wondered if he was an imported American thug. Since there was no answer, Bolt knocked again, louder. The Phantom waited expectantly. His long search was at an end. Now, the sacred image and Loka. So he thought.

"Open up," shouted Bolt impatiently. "What in hell are they doing in there? It's me, Bolt!"

There was a weak sound from inside, something like a groan, something like a cry for help. Bolt hurriedly pulled a ring of jangling keys from his pocket and unlocked the door.

The room had not changed since Diana fled. Gyp lay on the floor, breathing hard, staring at them. The twisted body of Helmsley was near the pool table. That was all. No girl, no Loka, no image. Bolt took it all in at a glance, then shouted at the gunman who stood in the doorway, his mouth wide open. "Shut the door!" He bent over Helmsley. "Dead," he muttered. He whirled to Gyp.

"What in hell's going on here?" he shouted, confused by this unexpected scene. Gyp gasped and tried to talk.

"The man's wounded. You going to leave him there?" asked

the Phantom.

"You pick him up," shouted Bolt. "Ed, keep your gun on him. If he makes a funny move, shoot him."

The gunman nodded, chewing his gum madly now, the gun pointed, as the Phantom knelt at Gyp's side and quickly examined his wound.

"Bullet wound . . . stomach . . . serious . . . could be worse . you'll live," he said to the Gypsy who stared at him. He lifted him carefully and placed him in the armchair (where Diana had been such a short time before). "You'd better call for an ambulance right away."

"Sure, with a police escort," snapped Bolt. He glared at Gyp. "What happened? Let's have it, Gyp," he commanded.

Gyp let him have it, in a hoarse whisper. How Helmsley had shot him and tried to take off with the thing . . . how Helmsley had fallen on the thing, and that did it. (The Phantom stiffened at that. Old Murph, Duke, now Helmsley. It seemed incredible—yet here it was. He could see the bloody stains on Helmsley's shirt. However accidental it seemed each time, was this ancient curse for real? Who could deny it now, no matter how it was explained?)

"He fell on it?" said Bolt, interrupting Gyp's story. "That's what did it?"

Gyp nodded.

For a moment. Bolt stood stunned, recalling the scene when he'd almost touched the image. He looked toward the stranger, wide-eyed. "That curse—is it real?"

The stranger shrugged. "Who can say?"

Bolt rushed to the bar, poured a glass of whiskey and gulped it down. He breathed deeply. His panic subsided.

"Go on, Gyp," he said. "What then? After he fell on the thing?"

Gyp continued his story. Black Loka had grabbed the image and run off with it. The American bird took off after him. There was a deal someplace that Helmsley had worked out—one million eight hundred thousand. He stopped, exhausted from talking.

"One million eight? Deal? Where?" Bolt shouted, shaking Gyp by the shoulder. The gypsy groaned.

"Easy, man," said the Phantom sharply. "He stopped bleeding. You'll start it again."

Bolt whirled on him, his face redder than usual. Events and people were buzzing about him like hornets. He was used to running his own show. He'd lost control here.

"I'm asking you for the last time," he shouted. The young gunman tightened his grip on the gun. "Who are you with the dog and . . . say, who's that bird? You . . ." he said, suddenly putting them together.

"What bird?" said the Phantom with a foreboding.

"The American bird. Where do you two fit in this thing?"
"How did she get here?"

"Him," said Gyp, weakly pointing to the dead man.

The gambler whirled back to Gyp. "What deal? Where is it? Come on, man!"

His anxiety made him careless as he stepped in front of the Phantom. For a moment, he was in' the line of fire, between the gunman and the Phantom. The moment was enough. The Phantom was behind him, powerful hands on his neck, using him as a shield.

'Tell him to drop the gun."

"No," yelled Bolt, twisting, trying to turn his body to one side. The startled gunman danced from one side to another, trying to find his target. But as he moved, the Phantom moved with his shield before him, the twisting, cursing, choking Bolt. The gambler was tall and wide and thick—big enough to shield even the Phantom. They went almost all the way around the pool table in a weird ballet—the Phantom holding and dragging Bolt, the gunman trying to dart around them, but not quickly enough.

'Tell him to put the gun on the pool table," the Phantom told the sweating gambler. He applied more pressure. Bolt felt and heard his neck bones crackle. The power in those hands was capable of tearing his head right off his shoulders, or so the terrified man imagined as he shrieked:

"Ed, put it down."

The gunman hesitated and made another rush.

More pressure, more crackle.

"Ed, you idiot, do it," choked Bolt as he was whirled around. "Now. Now!"

Bewildered, the gunman placed the gun on the green felt A split second later, it was in the Phantom's hand. He released Bolt, who slumped over the pool table.

"Put your coat on the table," the Phantom ordered. The gunman obeyed. The Phantom took two guns from the pockets. His own. They had frisked him in the car. "Sit on the floor." The gunman obeyed. Gyp watched all this, as the Phantom returned his own guns to their holsters and pocketed the third gun.

"You the man with the dog?" Gyp asked weakly.

"Was the girl all right?" said the Phantom. Gyp nodded. "Where did she go?" Gyp shrugged. As long as he didn't move, he seemed to have no pain. Another question from the man wearing the green sunglasses. "Where did Loka go?" Gyp clamped his lips together.

"Those two are not about to help you, Gyp. Your gun wound and that body mean trouble for them. If you tell me. I'll send for an ambulance before I go." He did not say what he'd do if Gyp didn't tell him. Gyp imagined the worst. (And wrongly. The Phantom would send for help in any case.) Instead of answering, Gyp pointed weakly to a white card on the floor. It had remained where Loka dropped it.

As the Phantom bent down to pick it up, Bolt, still at the pool table, glanced at his gunman. Together, they charged at the stranger's back. This, they quickly discovered, was a mistake. At the first sound of their movements, he whirled about. His iron fist moved in a blur, landing twice with distinct "clumps." The two men dropped as if hit with a sledgehammer.

He glanced at the card. "Seven Savile Place. Is that where they went?" Gyp nodded, staring at his fallen friends, then at the stranger. He'd never seen anyone hit so fast and so hard. The Phantom went to the bar and picked up the phone. "What's the address here?" Gyp's lips tightened. "You want an ambulance, or do you want to die here?" asked the Phantom quietly.

"Thirty-five forty-seven Shrewtonbury Court," said Gyp.

With the operator's help, the Phantom reached the police. "A fight at thirty-five forty-seven Shrewtonbury," he reported. "One dead, one wounded, two unconscious, thirty-five forty-seven Shrewtonbury." And he hung up before they could ask any questions.

He started for the door. Gyp groaned.

"What'll I tell them about him?" he said, pointing weakly to Helmsley. "We didn't do it."

"Tell them the truth."

"Will they believe it?"

"Try to sound convincing."

"Bolt'll be sore. Mister, will I be all right?"

But he was gone. The door remained ajar, saving the police the trouble of breaking it open when they arrived ten minutes later.

He hailed a cab, then stopped at the first phone booth and called Diana's hotel. Out. She'd left no message. He went on, blaming himself for having let Diana anywhere near this affair. He shuddered at the thought of her in that room, in the hands of those men. Where was she now? Safe somewhere, having tea, he hoped, but somehow, he knew that possibility was remote.

"His Highness is no longer here. His party checked out," the supercilious clerk with the white carnation told him.

"When?"

"Recently."

"Did a young woman, a Miss Palmer, come here?"

The clerk looked at him in annoyance. He was not at liberty to answer questions about guests.

"This is a police matter," said the Phantom to the bored man.

"Did she come here? Did she leave?"

"Without proper identification, we can't reveal such matters, sir. What branch are you?" he asked loftily.

The Phantom grasped him by his well-pressed lapels.

"Talk, man. Was she here? And a man named Loka, a black man?"

"Both," gasped the startled clerk. "They left—airport— not her."

"What do you mean, not her?" he said, shaking him.

"Didn't see her leave. Perhaps back stairs."

"What room?"

"Suite forty-nine . . ."

The doorman, noticing the argument, rushed in. But the Phantom had already left and galloped up the stairs. The clerk reached weakly for the phone and shouted into it, "Police!"

The Phantom climbed rapidly to the third floor. He regretted his rough tactics with the clerk, but the statement that Diana had entered but had not been seen to leave shook him. He refused to speculate on what might have happened. He just had to get to that suite fast. The door of 49 was closed and locked. He looked about anxiously for a housemaid, someone to unlock the door. There was no one. He broke it open with a single powerful shove, and burst into the suite calling "Diana . . . Diana."

He ran through the drawing room. The occupants had left recently, and the place had not been cleaned or straightened yet. There were little brass coffee cups, newspapers, trash in the wastebaskets. He raced through the four bedrooms that comprised the suite. All the rooms showed evidence of recent departure—spilled powder and towels on the bathroom floors, a comb forgotten or abandoned, plates with half- eaten food, an empty wine bottle, rumpled beds. He looked in every closet and under beds. No Diana anywhere. He looked out the windows. All opened on the busy street. If she'd been pushed out, it would be no secret.

Why had she come here? Chasing Loka and the image? Daring foolish girl, trying to help. He returned to the drawing room. The coffee set caught his eye, something on one of the cups. Red lipstick. He sniffed the cup, searching for her perfume. No trace of that, but something else, a faint lavender scent of a powerful drug he knew well. Someone, wearing lipstick, had been drugged to sleep. Diana? Where had they taken her? He realized he might be making all this up and that she could be on her way to her hotel at that very moment. And Loka and the image? Had he reached her with tit? Too many questions. No answers. He galloped down the stairs to the lobby. The clerk and doorman were together at the counter. They backed up as he rushed at them.

"Did any woman leave with the Sheik's party?"

"One," said the clerk, trying to edge behind the doorman.

"What did she look like?"

"Couldn't tell. In a wheelchair, her head covered with a veil," said the paunchy doorman, "Are you Scotland Yard, sir?"

"Wheelchair? Was a woman registered in the party?"

"That old bird had many a lady visitor. None registered," said the doorman with a toothless grin. "Mister, that lady you speak of, I paid her taxi fare."

"You what?"

"When she came here . . . lost her purse, she said. I often make advances for the guests—expecting, naturally, a tip, sir," he went on, winking broadly.

"How much?"

"Two quid," said the doorman with a straight face.

The Phantom handed him the money. "You didn't see her go?"

"Many's the time the ladies leave by the back way," he grinned. The clerk had remained frozen during all this.

"Now we'll see!" he announced suddenly. A police car was stopping at the curb. "They want to talk to you, sir."

The Phantom turned and raced through the lobby, into the lounge. A nice old woman, the ladies' room attendant, was standing there.

"Where's the back door?" She pointed the way. He raced on, out the door, into the alley, over a fence, across a yard, another fence, and he was gone.

On the way to the airport, he stopped the cab three times at as many phone booths, each time calling Diana's hotel. No answer in her room. No message for him. He reached Heathrow Airport. At the information booth, the pert girl in uniform advised him, after having the name spelled three times, and looking through two flight books, that no departures were scheduled for Suda-Kalara that day.

"Are you sure?"

"Positive."

That puzzled him for a moment. Had she seen a group with a man who looked like a Gulf Sheik? Dozens every day, she said with a grin. The place was full of them. But the Sheik of Suda-Kalara was not an ordinary type, he was one of the world's richest men. Would he use the scheduled airlines? Probably not, he quickly told himself. Either a charter, or his own plane. Where to find out about such flights? "Over there," said the pert girl, pointing to an office door.

Behind the door, a bald man with heavy eyebrows and a bushy mustache sat behind a desk reading a travel brochure extolling the beauties of the South Seas. Was there a non-scheduled plane flying to Suda-Kalara? The man examined a sheet. One item caught his eye. He studied it. Then he shook his head. "Such flights are confidential, for security reasons," he said, looking carefully at the big man wearing sunglasses. Men like the Sheik were protected at every step—by guards, by clerks, by bureaucrats. The Phantom was desperate. From the man's reaction, there obviously was, had been, or would be such a flight.

"I've no wish to assassinate the Sheik, or even borrow money from him. My girl is on that plane. I want to say good-bye," he said as lightly as he could. The man grinned.

"I'm not supposed to tell you and I'll deny it if you say I told you. Try Gate Thirty-two." He winked and went back to his travel folder.

He rushed to Gate 32. It was closed, locked. Beyond was an open door, through it the field. On the field, a large plane warming up. He looked around. A gateman was a few yards away. No use talking to him. The iron gate was about ten feet high. He grasped the bars, then swung up and over it, dropping to the other side in a flash. The gateman called to him, then rushed to a wall phone.

He ran through the door onto the field and headed for the big plane that was starting to roll. There were warning shouts behind him, the sound of running feet. He ran on, nearing the plane. High up in the small windows, several faces looked down at him. One, a bearded man wearing a turban with a shining jewel. A black man who had to be Lamanda's brother Loka. A big black shaven head, another face framed by a burnoose hood, and a shapeless head, covered in black. The faces looked down at him as he ran alongside the plane, calling a name—Diana. Then the jet motors revved up. A mighty blast hit him, knocking him off his feet. The plane rolled on, picking up speed. Two airport policemen rushed toward him. He got up and stared after the plane. It had reached the runway and was taking off.

"You're not permitted out here, sir. If you've suffered any injury, you cannot hold us responsible," said the officer.

"No injuries. I was just saying good-bye."

"This area is for departing passengers only," said the other officer sternly.

"Sorry, my mistake."

As he neared the door back into the building, he noticed something he had not seen on the way out—a wheelchair.

In the big plane, the Sheik and his aide looked curiously at the man running on the field, shouting up at them. Who might that be? Taras looked back at Loka, seated behind him with a big guard. "Did you know him?" Loka shook his head. In the next seat behind Loka, the figure in the black veils slumped against the window. The big guard with her moved her so that she lay back in the seat. Loka clutched the large leather case on his lap.

"Rest that on the floor," said Taras. "We have a long voyage ahead."

"I'll hold it," said Loka, clutching it tightly. It was all he had to hold on to. His mind was a blank, stunned by what was happening to him. The huge man who sat silently next to him had black skin like his own. That was all they had in common. Not one word of the same language. He could have been from a different age, a different planet. Slave. Slave? It couldn't be real. It can't be real. I'll wake up. It'll be a bad dream. I'll laugh when I tell Sala. But an icy clutching pain in his gut told him this was no dream. It was real.

CHAPTER 15

Suda-Kalara was a tiny landlocked kingdom deep in the great desert, and deeper into the Middle Ages. With no seaport, no shoreline or other access to the sea, it had remained completely cut off from the outside world for centuries. With only a scattering of oases, a few dreary dried-mud villages and miles of sand, it had had nothing to attract the conquerors from the days of the ancient Persians on. It was equally of no interest to Western travelers or the later hordes of tourists. It remained known only to its own disease-ridden inhabitants, a few roving Bedouin bands and the caravans.

Camel caravans still trekked across the sandy wastes. The swaying, ill-tempered "ships of the desert" carried goods for barter, still following the tradition of Biblical times. For Suda-Kalara, they also carried a commodity that was becoming rare in the twentieth century—slaves. Though outlawed by United Nations covenants and the laws of almost every nation on earth, the ancient evil persisted in a few remote areas—among them, Suda-Kalara.

Sometime after World War II, a revolutionary discovery was made there. The tiny kingdom rested on a sea of oil. And the Sheik, whose family had acquired all the real estate over the centuries, now owned all the oil. Personally. No one could accurately estimate his newfound wealth. With it, he bought all the luxurious products of the West—motorcars, planes, air conditioning, inside plumbing, and powerful weapons for his tiny army. The weapons were the only products purchased for use by anyone but himself. He had no intention of squandering his billions foolishly on such extravagances as hospitals, schools, housing, roads or all the rest of the things that some of his more enlightened fellow rulers were building or buying.

The Sheik Mustapha Ali Suda-Kalara was a traditionalist. Except for his new personal conveniences, he wanted his country unchanged. With the expensive new weapons, his borders were closed tighter than ever. Visitors were not welcome, in fact rarely permitted. Only the technicians involved with his oil fields were welcomed. But they were carefully segregated in guarded compounds, and no families were permitted, only the workers. Though they complained, their wages were so lavish that they accepted the restrictions, and couldn't wait until they had saved enough to get out.

One of the hallowed traditions the Sheik respected was slavery. Though he had power of life and death over slaves, as well as over his "free" subjects, he did not mistreat his slaves. They were never permitted outside the vast palace estates. Since they were better clothed and fed than the free citizens, and received better medical attention and food than those outside, it was advisable to keep the slaves from public view. The free citizens might get some ideas.

The slaves tended his estates. The prettier young females staffed his large harems. There were women of many colors, many nations. In his television programs too, the Sheik liked variety. Since there was no television station within a thousand miles, he built his own. The only television sets in the country were in his ten palaces, in the military barracks, and the compounds of the foreign technicians. The programs consisted of films from all countries, shown twenty-four hours a day. No commercials. A television addict's dream.

This was the place Diana and Loka were rapidly approaching in the Sheik's luxurious private plane. It was a large jet, the sort used for transoceanic travel. But it did not have the conventional seats and aisles. Instead, it was furnished like the drawing room of one of the Sheik's palaces— a few deep sofas, large cushions, thick rugs, rich hangings, only a few uncovered windows.

As Diana slept, a servant removed the black veil that covered her face. The Sheik and his aide Taras discussed her. Both held the medieval opinion of women that was common to males in their part of the world: Women were only good for pleasure or bearing children. The Sheik had known a few European women, and though he'd never known an American, he recognized that Diana had background and breeding. At first, it seemed a mistake that they had brought her. But time had been short, and since he'd decided to take the image, he could not leave her behind. There was the fact of Helmsley's death—a nuisance. And the stolen art object. The Sheik valued the respect of his fellow rulers. It would not do to be involved in such shoddy matters.

What to do with this sleeping girl? She was bound to be missed, by someone. Seven Savile Place might remember her visit, though they hadn't seen her leave with them. The Sheik shrugged at all this. He had no sense of lawbreaking. He was the law in his land. There was only the fear of offending his peers in neighboring countries as well as in the United Nations which he had recently joined. Obviously, the girl's presence must be kept a secret. The Sheik observed her with the eyes of an expert. Even drugged and asleep, she was pretty. Well made. In proper attire, she would even be beautiful. The solution was simple. She would disappear into his vast harem. At first, as was customary, she would remain close to him. Later, she would go to the officers' barracks.

When Diana awoke, it took her time to realize what had happened. When she did, her first reaction was anger, fury. But there was no comfort in the cold faces around her. Only the anxious eyes of Loka watched with fear and sadness. They did not tell her why she had been brought along, or where she was going. They told her nothing. She would learn all in due time. The Sheik had retired to his private chamber on the plane and was not present when she awoke. Taras advised her to sit quietly, or she would be tied up.

Her anger, soon changed to despair. The Phantom? What could he be thinking? If only she had called her hotel and left a message for him as she wanted to! That would have given her some hope. But now, how could he ever find her? How could he know that she had actually been abducted, and was being flown to some unknown destination—most likely the Sheik's country. While she had waited that short time in the lounge of 7 Savile Place, her hand had actually been on the phone. She had been about to phone her hotel and leave the message for him. But the phone had rung at that very second, the desk clerk telling her to go upstairs—"at once." She clenched her fists. If only she had waited a moment, made that call. If . . . If. . . . She sank back into the deep seat. The huge black guard near her was like a statue. What now? What now?

At the desert airport, a cordon of soldiers surrounded the big plane. Diana was once more covered with the heavy black veil. She and Loka, clutching the box, were whisked into a big limousine with curtained windows, along with the two giant guards. The Sheik and Taras rode in a specially built Rolls Royce—the entire top was transparent, bulletproof plastic, giving him a clear, safe view of his beloved subjects, and vice versa.

They reached the Sheik's main palace, a vast complex of gardens, fountains, pavilions and buildings that rivaled the Taj Mahal in beauty and the French palace at Versailles for size. Beautiful and enormous. Its furnishings and art treasures staggered the imagination. The wealth of the world was pouring into this tiny, remote kingdom, and much of it was in this palace.

Diana, still veiled, was walked and carried (when she started to resist) into the heavily guarded women's quarters. There, a quartet of fat women stripped off her clothes, giggling and chattering all the while. At first, Diana tried to fight them off. It was useless. They were as strong as men. When she realized they were trying to get her into a huge bathtub, she relaxed. The warm perfumed water covered with blossoms looked delicious. She was dying for a bath. These women were the working staff of the harem. Not the sex objects. A few of those beauties in scanty gauzy attire watched at a distance. The word "Amerikane" was whispered among them and raced through the quarters. More girls of all sizes and ages joined the spectators. There were women of many races and nations here, some from Western Europe. This one was a rarity, a genuine Amerikane!

Then, bathed, dried, powdered and perfumed, she was clad in a wispy garment like the others (like a strip-teaser near the end of her act, thought Diana). A jeweled necklace, then jangling bracelets on her arms and ankles. She was led to a big cushion and seated there, while one of the fat women brushed her hair. Then she was left alone. After a few moments, some of the other harem girls approached her shyly and spoke to her in several languages, none of which she understood. She looked at the smiling, pretty, dull-eyed faces. I can't believe this, she told herself. I'm in a real harem! Now what?

Loka was brought into a large chamber, the throne room. Taras instructed him to place the image on a marble table. Soon many people, both men and women, assembled. They were the entire palace staff. Armed guards stood at the doors. They saluted smartly as the Sheik entered, clad in sparkling white from head to toe—turban, silk jacket and baggy pants, leather boots with curling tips. He stood before his azure and gold throne and told them about the image that no one save Loka on pain of death was ever to touch. They understood. They bowed. They left. A bench was placed near the image. Taras told Loka he was to sit there every day, all day, except when eating or sleeping. He was in charge of the image, polishing it, watching it. The armed soldiers, at their normal posts at the doorways, would also guard it.

Loka sank down on the bench. By now, he understood his role and his fate. All day always. He was a slave, the lowest of the low. He would live and die here, a slave. There could be no escape from this heavily guarded place. None, except death. He was right about that. There was no escape from the entire small country. There was no place to go. He thought of Sala, fierce, loyal, beautiful Sala, as devoted as though she were his slave. How stupid he had been to leave her with that ship's captain! Duke had insisted she be left behind. No women. He thought of his shack where he and Sala had spent so many happy hours. He thought of his village—the huts, the happiness. He thought of his brother . . . high up in his own palace. What a fool I was, he cried to himself, the eternal plaint of the prodigal. He stared at the sacred image, gleaming so brightly under the hundreds of chandelier bulbs. This is what had brought his people good luck? He was Llongo. Where was his luck? What had it done for him? Brought him to this shameful state. No Llongo in all history had ever been a slave. In the days of the slave trade, they'd fought to the death rather than be put in chains. But here he was, nephew of the High Chief, brother of the most important man in the nation, a slave to the image he had stolen from his own people. Some luck!

Deep in his misery, Loka could not know that his luck was on the way at last, riding high above the clouds, moving faster than the wind.

CHAPTER 16

Before leaving Heathrow Airport, the Phantom learned that he could make a connection to Suda-Kalara the following day by changing planes in Rome. He returned to Diana's hotel and waited for several hours. There was a slim chance she had slipped out of 7 Savile Place and was still in London. Her clothes were still neatly arranged in her suitcase, her toilet articles on the bureau. He looked at them with a heavy heart. If she was still in London, was she alive? He made a few phone calls to hospitals, police stations, and finally, to the morgue. No information about her. That done, he knew what he must do. Go to Suda-Kalara. Either she was there, or the information about her was there. And Loka and the sacred image were also there. He checked Diana out of the hotel, taking her suitcase.

He sent two long cables, one to Bangalla, one to New York. Then he went to the kennels to get Devil. The big gray wolf was so overjoyed to see him that he almost knocked down the attendant who led him out of his cage. Outside the airport, he had a porter take Devil to the freight section. The police might still be watching for a man with a dog like Devil. He had checked the freight section of the plane to Rome. The pressure and temperature were the same as the passenger section. Devil would be comfortable there.

That was not true of the plane leaving Rome, so Devil joined him in the passenger section after some palaver at the plane's ramp.

The same objections were made as before, but the Phantom won the argument, as he had before. As one of the watching stewardesses, a dark-skinned beauty, observed, "He's a man it's hard to say no to." She out-maneuvered the two other stewardesses and served him both dinner and breakfast, as well as raw hamburger for his dog (?). But she couldn't get him to remove either hat or topcoat. A man of mystery. It was with much regret that she watched him get off at the funny little airport at Suda-whatever-it-was . . . a place hardly anybody ever went to.

At the customs shed, an officer in a colorful uniform asked for his passport. It was issued to one Kit Walker, a gentleman (no profession) residing in Bangalla. Lamanda Luaga had gotten it for him long ago to facilitate his travel. Ordinarily, the Phantom ignored such conventions, slipping across borders like the wind. But the passport didn't help here. The officer scowled, and asked his business. The Phantom did not hesitate, but made a bold move. He was here to! see the Sheik on business. That impressed the officer. He told him to wait while he went to a tiny office to make a phone call. There was only one other man in sight, a sleepy-eyed soldier with a rifle at the exit. Several other soldiers were on the field, flirting with the stewardesses. It was still an erotic experience for them to see a bare-faced woman.

The Phantom moved quickly to the exit. The officer at the phone saw this and shouted. The sleepy soldier woke up but not fast enough, as a hard fist crashed on his jaw. The officer rushed out, cursing, drawing a pistol from his belt holster and firing. But the Phantom was no longer in the shed. There was a small army vehicle parked outside, an open model patterned after an American jeep. Such cars are not usually locked. This one was no exception. By the time the other soldiers, attracted by the gunfire, had rushed in, he was a mile down the smooth eight-lane highway, headed for the distant minarets and towers that looked like an entire city but were in fact the Sheik's palace grounds.

Speeding along on the roadway, the Phantom was amused. The highway was equal to the biggest autobahns in Europe or the American parkways. Not a car in sight. Probably used only by the military and the Sheik's retinue of cars. He looked back. Several cars were speeding after him. He pressed the gas pedal to the floorboard. Devil stood up on the seat, enjoying the wind. Soon, he passed huge iron gates, with guards inside and out. They glanced at him as he sped by. He followed the wall, which curved for a mile beyond the gate, then stopped.

The wall was about ten feet high, topped with spikes. Standing on the hood of his car, he lifted Devil up carefully, so that his paws landed between the spikes, then told him to jump. Devil jumped. The Phantom tossed Diana's suitcase over the wall, then leaped up front the hood, reaching the spikes and pulling himself up. He had no idea what was on the other side. But as the pursuing vehicles roared up, he vaulted over the wall and landed in thick flowering bushes.

Devil had landed in the same bushes and had worked his way out. Ahead were lawns and gardens that seemed endless, presided over by rows of revolving water sprinklers. The sudden view of lush green grass, trees, bushes and flowerbeds after the dry desert was startling. In the distance beyond this greenery were the white walls of buildings, the towers and minarets he had seen. Outside the wall, he heard the roar of the cars and the screech of brakes. Then excited voices and some scratching on the wall, as his pursuers tried to climb up. They quit, the motors revved up and sped off, probably back to those big gates.

He quickly shed his outer clothing, leaving it piled on Diana's suitcase. He could move easier and faster unencumbered by the hat, coat, trousers. Once more the masked, hooded figure, he crawled through the bushes with Devil following closely. No one was in sight. Evidently no one inside had seen him jump from the wall. But the soldiers would be at the main gate by now, rushing here to find him.

He dashed across open lawn to another clump of bushes, then across another open space to a small building that looked like a tool shed, and was. Not a good hiding place. They'd certainly look there. Near the shed was a high tree bearing heavy foliage. Devil was a problem, the soldiers would doubtless shoot him on sight. There were some old sacks in the shed. On command, Devil curled up in a corner. The Phantom covered him. Devil made a small mound, too small to be a man. To complete the hiding place, he placed two flowerpots on the sacks. In the dark shed, Devil could now be a mound of earth, covered with sacks, topped with flowerpots. The Phantom quickly climbed onto the roof of the shed, leaped up into the tree, and concealed himself among the leafy branches thirty feet in the air.

Soon soldiers appeared from several directions, headed for the place where he'd come over the wall. There were a dozen men, and they poked with their rifles through the bushes near the wall. One shouted excitedly. He'd found the suitcase and the clothes. He ran toward the buildings with his find. The others continued the search, poking through clumps of bushes. Two of them approached the shed cautiously, rifles poised. The door was open. That made it scarcely worth looking into. First the two carefully circled the shed, meeting at the back. One peered into the shed, shouted to his partner, and they went on. The soldiers spread out farther and farther in this vast garden, their voices becoming fainter as they called to each other.

One wandered back, looked about cautiously, then sat behind the shed and lit a cigarette. From above, the Phantom watched with amusement. The soldier was breaking a rule, smoking on duty. He settled back against the shed, blowing smoke rings, then idly glanced up. The cigarette fell from his mouth. He'd seen the figure above. He jumped to his feet, grabbing his rifle. At the same moment, the Phantom dropped twenty feet to a heavy bough, caught hold of it briefly to break his fall, then dropped the rest of the distance to the ground. Just as the soldier raised his rifle, the Phantom landed on him. The soldier fell to the grass. A strong hand clapped over his mouth. He was dragged into the shed. Devil squirmed out from under the sacks, upsetting the flowerpots. The soldier stared in terror at this beast with its long slavering fangs. Devil was slavering because he was hot and thirsty. Also panting, for the same reason. In the dim light, the soldier could barely make out his captor, a strange masked figure. To say he was terrified would be a mild understatement. He was paralyzed with fear, barely able to hear or answer the questions put to him in his own tongue. The Phantom was fluent in a dozen languages, including the basic speech of the desert people.

"What is this place?"

The strong hand was removed from his mouth so he could answer. He started to shout. The hand gripped his throat. He almost blacked out. The question was repeated.

"The palace," he replied.

"Of the Sheik."

"Yes."

"Is he here now?"

The soldier nodded, still terrified by the hot breath and gleaming fangs of the hairy beast that was only a foot from his face in the narrow confines of the shed.

"Did an American girl come with him?"

The soldier mumbled that he didn't know. Then in sudden panic, he tried to twist out of the iron grip that held him.

As he was to relate later, that's all he remembered. When he came to, he had an aching jaw and something else that went with it. Perhaps he'd been hit. He had been—with a quick sharp blow.

The Phantom peered outside. No one in sight. He sped across the lawns, back to the thick bushes near the wall where he had entered the palace grounds. Devil was at his heels. It was unlikely that the soldiers would search here again. He looked toward the palace, far in the background. The sound of tinkling music and feminine laughter floated on the air that was perfumed by thousands of flowering bushes and trees. Water splashed in the many fountains. Like all desert people, they treasured fountains. Under other circumstances, a lovely place to be. Was Diana in the palace? Was she still alive? He had no way of knowing. He would wait until dark to find out. He wondered about the music and laughter—life as usual in this fantastic place? How odd, he thought. Hadn't word reached the palace yet that a stranger, a possible assassin, was hidden inside the wall, on the grounds? Even as he thought about this, the music and laughter stopped suddenly, as if at the wave of a conductor's baton. They'd gotten the news about the possible assassin— about him.

CHAPTER 17

At first, the report circulated slowly, from airport security to the military and the police bureau. A stranger had made an illegal entry, a man with a dog. It was nothing to get excited about. He was obviously mad. Where could a stranger like this, a European type, hide among the desert people of tiny Suda-Kalara? Every row of houses and shanties had its police spy. There were no secrets in this tightly controlled kingdom. Only in the compounds of the foreign technicians could he try to find refuge. But these places were also well supplied with informers. No chance there. But by the time the report reached the palace security office, the stranger had already climbed over the palace wall and disappeared.

In the guards' cellar barracks, alarms sounded. Armed men rushed through the corridors, doubling the guards already there, both inside and outside the palace. Even the Sheik, surrounded by laughing harem beauties and singing dancing girls noticed the excitement. His lifted eyebrow sent Taras running out to find what was happening.

Loka watched with dull eyes. The Sheik had him place the image on the floor near him, so that he could gloat over it as he gurgled and bubbled on a waterpipe. He told the girls about this rare treasure. They ohed and ahed over it, and one red-haired beauty almost touched it. The Sheik stopped her, warning that it could jump at her. This amused the beauties, and they swayed and danced about the image, laughing and singing.

Taras returned, his face tense. The laughter and merriment was at its height as he bent over the Sheik and whispered in his ear. The Sheik waved his hand in an angry gesture. The sounds in the large chamber stopped instantly, as though the needle had been lifted off a record. Taras sent the girls out of the room. Without question, or reaction, they obeyed automatically, rushing out on bare feet, the little bells tinkling on their ankles and wrists.

"Loka," said Taras sternly. "Who is the man with the dog?"

Loka stared stupidly, stirred out of a deep reverie about his homeland, about his hopeless existence here. By now he was resigned to his station in life. Within a short time, slavery had become a way of life. His Western clothes were gone. He was bare to the waist, with baggy pants and sandals, like the other palace slaves. He looked dumbly at Taras. The aide walked to him and shook his shoulder.

"In London, the man with the dog we heard about. Who is he?"

Loka was so sunk in shock and apathy, so depressed, that he barely remembered London or the events of that violent day.

"Man with dog?" he said dully. "Don't know."

"You know. Tell us or you will be whipped."

Loka's eyes filled with fear. He had been whipped by one of the giant guards that morning, merely because he had refused to finish his breakfast, a coarse gruel. The Sheik wanted his slaves to eat well, to remain strong. It was a mild beating for a first offense, he'd been told. Mild? His body still ached hours afterwards. He didn't want to be whipped again, even mildly.

"Man with dog. I only heard of him," he said with difficulty, "from the newspaper. I never saw him."

"That's not good enough, Loka. We believe this man has followed us," said Taras. The Sheik watched intently, gurgling and bubbling on his waterpipe. Loka tried to look interested, but the matter apparently meant nothing to him— unless he was a superb actor, which Taras doubted.

"We believe that man, and the dog, are near—on the palace grounds. We will find him, of course," continued Taras. Loka nodded, hoping the subject was closed, and with it any reason for the whip.

"Loka, there is something curious here," continued Taras in a puzzled voice. 'This man struck down a soldier at the airport. The man was left with a mark on his jaw, like a skull mark."

"Skull mark?"

"Death's head. Like the head of a skeleton. Does that mean anything to you?"

Loka stared at his masters. The dull look was gone from his eyes. They blazed. Then the strangest thing of all happened. He laughed. No slave had ever laughed before his master in the history of Suda-Kalara. Taras motioned to the nearby guards to approach. The man was obviously losing his mind, and the words that followed confirmed it.

"He is the Phantom—the Ghost Who Walks—the Man Who Cannot Die," he shouted, his words coming so fast they were almost incoherent. "Dog? That is no dog. That is his wolf. Devil, the great wolf. You are doomed," he cried.

If Loka sounded mad, his mind was working with rapid clarity. Suddenly, many things made sense. Something, someone had been trailing him and the image, ever since he left Bangalla. The man who had found Duke, the man who had fled over the rooftops, the man the girl had talked about in the Sheik's suite. What had she called him—"a law enforcer from Bangalla."

The guards had grabbed his arms. The Sheik nodded sternly. "Take him out and beat him," said Taras. "It is a good old-fashioned cure for madness."

"You will see. You will see," Loka shouted as they dragged him to the door. "You are doomed . . . the Ghost Who Walks." One of the guards cuffed Mm hard, and he was silent as they left the chamber. The Sheik looked at Taras inquiringly. He had no fear. A would-be assassin on the grounds? He had a thousand guards inside the walls.

"There is a man on the grounds, sire, with a dog."

The Sheik shrugged. "Find him. I am bored. Bring the singers and dancers back. Oh, the image. Put it. . ."

Taras bent toward the gleaming image, then paused and looked questioningly at his master.

"Leave it," said the Sheik.

"Highness, we should not neglect this matter. It may be important," said Taras.

"What is your suggestion, Taras?"

"The girl, Diana, knew the man with the dog. We should question her."

"Of course," said the Sheik impatiently. "That is a police matter. Let them interrogate her, but not before I have seen her," he added, smiling. "She may dine with me this evening." The Sheik's word "may" was a command. Taras bowed and was about to leave, when an officer of the guard entered to report that a soldier had been found in a garden shed, unconscious, with an odd mark on his jaw. Perhaps the work of the stranger.

"What kind of a mark?" said Taras quickly.

"Something like a skull mark, sire."

"Bring him in here," said the Sheik.

He gurgled on his waterpipe, annoyed that he was being denied the pleasures of his dancing girls. But the mysterious mark intrigued him. The man was carried in, his uniform covered with fertilizer from the garden shed. He was placed on the floor before the Sheik, near the image. He was breathing, alive, but had been hit hard. The jaw was swollen. On it was the mark. It was clearly what they said it was—a death's head.

"It won't wash off," said the captain of the guard. Normally a stolid man, he seemed unusually upset.

"Well, Captain?" said Taras.

"I sailed for several years, sire. I . . . I heard of that mark."

"What did you hear?" said Taras.

The man appeared embarrassed.

"Up and down the Gulf, on the Indian Ocean and the China Seas, as well as the West Coast and the Atlantic, all these places I have sailed," he said hesitantly.

"Get on with it," said Taras sharply.

"That mark is well known to all seamen. I heard many tales in my time," he said, looking fearfully at the Sheik who watched him sharply.

"It is the mark of the Phantom, sire, called by some the Ghost Who Walks," he said.

"And why do they call him that?" said the Sheik suddenly.

"Highness, I never saw him, but I've met those who have. I saw that mark once, on a dock worker in Maracas, said to have been a pirate in the China Seas."

"Captain, you haven't answered his Highness's question," said Taras slowly, as though not really wishing to hear the answer.

"He is called what I said because he is the Man Who Cannot Die. He has lived, they say, over four hundred years. He lives today. That is his mark," said the captain, his voice suddenly frantic.

"Captain, control yourself. You will not repeat this nonsense. If we hear any more of this ridiculous talk, you will be reduced to the ranks. Is that clear?" said Taras. The captain nodded stiffly, coming to attention, his face impassive. "Good. Get him out of here. When he revives, find out who did it, and report to me."

The guards and captain carried the unconscious soldier out of the chamber. The Sheik looked at Taras with his usual questioning expression—a lifted eyebrow.

"Superstition, obviously," said Taras.

"And is that also superstition?" said the Sheik, glancing at the sacred image. "Bring the girl here at once. Diana?"

"Palmer," said Taras.

"Palmer," said the Sheik, relishing the odd name.

Seated on cushions, Diana attracted a large audience of the harem girls, who were curious about her and her country. One spoke passable French, another knew some Italian, and one a little English. Since Diana was fluent in all three languages, she was able to talk to them. And they served as interpreters for the others. The girls wanted to know about American men, Hollywood, and skyscrapers. And Diana wanted to know about the girls, where they came from, how they had gotten here. The information was exchanged with much laughter. Nearby, two huge eunuch guards, fat beardless men with squeaky voices, watched without interest, sleepy and bored, thinking only of the next meal.

Diana was surprised to learn that the girls, by and large, were not in this harem against their will, or as a result of white (or nonwhite) slavers. Most of them came from impoverished villages and homes. The Sheik's agents made the rounds annually, seeking the prettiest girls. A deal would be made with their families. It was considered an honor to be chosen for the Sheik's harem. It also meant food, clothes and shelter for the lucky girl and cash for her poor family. For their part, the girls were amazed to learn that in Amerikka (as they pronounced it) men had only one wife. Their comments about this were hilarious, accompanied with much tittering and tinkling of bells. So it went, and Diana laughed too, feeling like a tourist in this exotic place and forgetting for a time that she was an inmate.

But as night came and the servants moved quietly about turning on soft lamps and lighting candles, two guards appeared outside the bronze grille doors. The big eunuchs moved to the laughing group and told Diana to accompany them. The girls translated. Diana froze, all the laughter gone. Now what? She refused to move. While the girls, now silent, made way and watched, the big fat man picked her up and carried her to the entrance.

"I can walk," she cried angrily, getting her feet to the floor. "Where are they taking me?" she called to the girls. One of them ran to her, smiling.

"Do not be afraid. They will not hurt you. They are taking you to the master."

The bronze gates of the harem clanged behind her.

As the lights from the palace began to flicker through the darkness, the Phantom and Devil moved out of the bushes. Search parties had been trooping by for hours, and he'd changed hiding places twice. But so adept at cover were they that they were unnoticed. In the jungle, if upwind, both were able to lie concealed, soundless and motionless, while a great cat passed close to them. How much simpler to hide from the noisy thrashing soldiers. Now, with the coming of nightfall, guards moved only near the palace, where the lights were on. But in the dark garden, he knew others were concealed, in bushes, behind pavilions and sheds.

With Devil, he moved slowly toward the palace on all fours. It was like going through a mined field at night, except he now had to avoid riflemen instead of mines. As they approached a nearby clump of bushes, Devil stopped and flattened on the grass, his long nose pointing toward the bushes. The Phantom also lay flat on the grass, and wriggled to the bushes. Reaching them, he made out the vague form of a soldier in the pale starlight. A quick karate chop followed by a swift blow to the jaw, and the soldier fell without a sound. This slow approach was repeated four times. Each time, Devil halted, flattened, and pointed, his keen nose and ears picking up the presence of the hidden guard. And each time the Phantom reached the man and silenced him before he could make an outcry.

Now he reached the flowerbeds alongside a wide veranda. Across the veranda were high glass doors stretching from floor to ceiling. Gauzy draperies covered the windows, and soft music came from inside, a modem French ballad, either on a record or from the radio station. As he crouched by the railing, Devil suddenly alerted him, pointing to the side. A squad of soldiers was approaching. He had to decide either to retreat into the dark garden and lose all the headway he had made, or enter the palace. He made the decision in a flash, leaped over the railing with Devil, quietly opened the high door and slipped inside.

The scene was one of Oriental splendor. A long wide room with a low ceiling. Rich wall hangings of gold and silver cloth. Flowers and greenery in dozens of vases. Soft lamps and candlelight. Beautiful tiled floors. A long pool with gleaming emerald-green water. And seated about and near the pool on cushions, eating from low tables, were dozens of women in scanty gauzy costumes. There was a low hum of conversation as all concentrated on their food. As he entered quietly with Devil, the girl nearest him gasped. All heads turned in his direction. He had a fleeting impression of young pretty faces in this dim light. It might have been a dining room in a women's college, but he realized where he was. The Sheik's harem.

For a moment, the girls stared at this masked apparition out of the night, and at the big hairy beast. Then several Shrieked and some started to their feet. In one corner, the huge eunuch guards were so intent on their food that they failed to look up for several seconds, enough time for the Phantom to move swiftly to the bronze gates. But they were bolted from the outside. One of the guards looked up, climbed laboriously to his feet, and drew a long scimitar that hung from his belt. He lumbered toward the intruder with the big weapon raised over his head. He had no intention of asking who this man was. Masked or not masked, a man in the harem was a disaster.

Devil crouched, ready to leap. The Phantom stopped him

with a quick command and waited, poised in a wrestler's stance. For a moment, the girls were frozen into silence, watching their protector (and jailer) advance on the stranger. The Phantom did not draw his guns. He waited. As the man swung clumsily at him, he ducked under the weapon with ease, grasped the obese guard, lifted him into the air, and hurled him into the pool. He made an enormous splash, such as a small whale might make.

The action was so unexpected and funny that the girls exploded with laughter. They knew this guard well, and this was probably something they'd all dreamed of doing. Seeing this, the other fat eunuch retreated rapidly to the far end of the long chamber and reached for a wall phone.

Now, as the man in the pool flailed his arms and tried to reach the side, the girls stared at the stranger. A big powerful young man, such as they dreamed about during their lonely hours in this place. His nonviolent action with the fat man had reassured them. What did he want?

He put a finger to his lips and shushed them, a worldwide sign and sound known in any language.

"The American girl, is she here?" he said softly, but in a loud whisper all could hear, using the basic desert language.

The girls whispered excitedly to each other. So that is what this man wanted! The American girl. He was her lover. He had come to rescue her from the harem. This was a dream each had—a young lover who would suddenly appear in the night, overcome the guards, take her in his arms, and disappear into the night. Here he was, in the flesh. And masked as well, in a strange skintight costume that made him even more exciting. And with him, that great hairy beast that obeyed his slightest command. These lonely girls, with nothing else to think of all day except romance, fell in love with this daring intruder en masse. They clustered around him, all talking in excited whispers, anxious to help him find his love . . . the American; He was surrounded by bright eyes, smiling lips, perfumed skin, tinkling bells. In a dozen dialects, they told him where his loved one was—with the master.

He quickly questioned the girls nearest him, as the others crowded about trying to touch him, the way girls in other countries might surround a singing idol. Devil crawled out of the way of these tinkling bare feet and watched, his head cocked to one side.

"The American, was her name Diana?" he asked.

"Yes, Diana, Diana," a half dozen voices assured him.

A great load was lifted from him. His gamble had won. She was alive! She was here! One more question.

"The sacred image—the bull with two heads—is that here?"

"It is, it is. But no one may touch it," they warned him,

anxious that he shouldn't.

He was touched by their friendliness and amused by their conspiratorial tone, siding with him, wanting to help him. How quickly women understood such things, he told himself.

This conversation had happened quickly. They had forgotten about their ponderous guards, the one in the pool, and the second one who had disappeared someplace. The Phantom hadn't forgotten. He watched alertly as he talked, as alertly as he could with the crowd of swaying bodies and waving arms about him, whispering, laughing, warning, admiring. There was a low growl from Devil, heard only by the Phantom above the murmuring girls. A sound of metal as the bronze gates were unbolted. The girls gasped in unison and started to scatter as three soldiers with rifles swung open the heavy gates.

The Phantom looked about quickly. He had lost time here with the girls, but he had learned what he had to learn. There was no immediate escape route. Without hesitation, he spread his arms so that they touched three or four girls on either side and moved rapidly to the pool. A dozen girls were propelled with them as he jumped into the pool, pulling them with him.

There was pandemonium in the harem as the others ran every which way, screaming. And the dozen girls in the pool, waving their arms, splashing, gasping, trying to keep their heads above the surface. The amazed soldiers ran to the edge of the pool, trying to spot the big stranger whom they had glimpsed only briefly. He wasn't in sight. He was somewhere underwater, among the thrashing bodies.

The big eunuch guard who had preceded them into the pool had almost worked his way to the side, too fat to sink. A half dozen girls clambered over him, hanging onto his huge bulk, like shipwrecked people clinging to a raft.

The soldiers separated, covering three sides of the pool, searching. Meanwhile, the Phantom was swimming underwater, among the girls who were weaving wildly above him. He popped to the surface for a split second behind the mound of the eunuch, saw the soldiers' positions, ducked back under, swam to the end near the gates and leaped out. Only one soldier near him saw this. The others had their backs to him. As the soldier raised his rifle and started to shoot, he was hit hard from behind as Devil landed against him. The unexpected blow pushed him headfirst into the pool. The other soldiers turned. They had a brief glimpse of the stranger dashing out through the bronze gates, followed by a long gray streak. The gates clanged. The two soldiers rushed to the gates to find them bolted. They were locked in.

CHAPTER 18

As Diana was led into the large chamber, she expected the worst. That would be soft lights and music, and an amorously aggressive Sheik. The Sheik was waiting, but not as she imagined. He was seated on the low broad ottoman that served as a throne, and he puffed on his waterpipe. He looked at her with no change of expression. Taras, the aide who'd come with them from London, was also waiting. And on the floor, the gleaming image. The guards released her arms and remained at the entrance. She stood in the middle of the room as the men looked at her. This was the first time they'd seen her in the harem finery. She felt half-dressed, but she was too angry to care.

"Your Highness," she began angrily, "this nonsense has gone far enough."

"Quiet, girl," said Taras. "You will speak when spoken to. You will answer questions." But Diana was not ready to be bluffed.

"There are still laws in this world, even here. If you think you're beyond the law, you're crazy!" she said loudly, suddenly realizing that in this man's country, she was talking nonsense. Taras confirmed this quickly.

"Law? His word is law. Nothing else counts here, Miss Palmer." The Sheik nodded. "We have a question. You will answer it truthfully," continued Taras.

"You evaded this question in London. Now, we want a true

answer."

What could he be talking about? Diana wondered.

"Who is the man with the dog?"

Diana almost laughed. Why would they want to know that?

"In London, I imagine two million men have dogs," she said lightly. Taras walked to her; and surprised her by slapping her face. Not a brutal blow, but a sharp slap such as one might give to a naughty child. She flushed.

"Answer," he said angrily.

"I told you. He is a law enforcer."

"His name is Walker. He followed us from London. He is here," said Taras, watching her closely. Diana showed her amazement, then her overwhelming joy. She almost shouted with relief. Here! An end to this nightmare!

"Here? Where?" was all she managed to say.

"Diana," said the Sheik, pronouncing her name slowly, as though the sound pleased him, "what does the word 'Phantom' mean to you?"

Diana caught herself. She must be careful. What was this leading to?

"Phantom? In my language, it means a ghost," she replied.

"Yes, indeed. Does it mean Ghost Who Walks?"

"I don't know what you mean," she said, thinking she'd said enough. Taras raised his hand to slap her again. She clutched her cheek. The Sheik shook his head. Taras stepped back.

"And the skull mark—the death's head. What does that mean, Diana?" continued the Sheik, saying her name slowly as though it tasted good. They'd seen his mark someplace. That meant he was here, and that they hadn't found him yet, she told herself.

"You'd best ask him," she said with some spirit.

The Sheik nodded and smiled. "Capital suggestion, my dear Diana," again rolling the name slowly. He turned to Taras and spoke rapidly in his own tongue, saying that when they found the man, he wanted to see him before he was killed. Then he nodded abruptly. Taras bowed and backed out of the room. The guards on the doorway followed and shut the high doors. She was alone with the ruler. His grim look was gone. His expression softened. He smiled.

"Come here, my dear," he said, waving to the broad ottoman.

Oh, no, thought Diana. Here it comes. The soft lights and music.

He was intrigued with this American girl. She was not the usual sort that made up his harem. She was a lady of position and education, the sort that he met at embassy functions or at parties in Europe. She would be different.

"I'd rather stand," said Diana.

This further intrigued him. His women obeyed his slightest wish, like well-trained pets. This one was different. He was to find out how very different, in a moment.

"Indeed?" he said and stood up.

He approached her slowly, eying her from head to foot, smiling confidently. She stood her ground, angered by his manner. When he reached her, he looked intently at her. She did not flinch.

Where another man might have tried to soothe her with flattery, he felt no need to do so. Like Loka and all the rest, she belonged to him now. Without warning, he suddenly grabbed her in a tight bear hug. Diana reacted instantly, almost without thinking. The stunned Sheik flew over her shoulder and landed flat on his back on the polished floor with a loud thump. He fell within a few feet of the sharp horns of the gleaming image. His breath was knocked out of him. He stared from the floor, speechless. It should be mentioned that after a few judo lessons from the Phantom, Diana had gone on in New York to earn a first degree black belt.

Breathing hard, the Sheik got to his hands and knees, his head lowered. In all his life, he'd never suffered such humiliation. He couldn't believe this had happened to him, that he was on the floor, his back and head aching, on his knees before this woman. That she had dared! It was all beyond thought. He was filled with rage. When he lifted his head to look at her, the hatred in his face frightened her. But she held her ground.

"I am not sorry," she said. "You—you had no right to bring me here." She realized her protests were weak before this kneeling tyrant who held the power of life and death in this country. She knew what she had done was considered Unpardonable. She also knew that if she had to do it over again, she would do the same thing.

A growl came from the Sheik. He was trying to say something, but was so furious that his words choked in his throat. His face was crimson, his eyes popping, he was gulping for air. She watched him, appalled. He started to shriek for his guards, then stopped. It was obvious to her what he was thinking. His men could not be allowed to see him like this. He started to get up, but his back was strained from the hard fall. He began to crawl, near the image. Even in his incoherent rage, he stared at the sharp horns. He had almost fallen on them. She watched, terrified now, as he crawled like a huge glittering insect toward his low gold and azure throne. When he reached it, he pulled himself painfully upon it, then turned. He was glaring at her, like a madman. He breathed deeply.

"Guards! Guards!" he shrieked in a high falsetto.

The guards in the corridor, two of them, opened the huge doors and rushed in. They had heard the sound of the falling body from outside and grinned at each other. They hadn't realized it was him. Now they looked puzzled at their ruler half sprawled on the throne, his turban on the floor. He pointed with a shaking hand toward Diana.

"Take her! Take her!" he screamed in the same hysterical voice. "Take her out! Shoot the . . ." he finished with a filthy local slang word. Diana didn't understand the language, but she understood the intention. She tensed as the guards grabbed her arms.

"You will be killed—you understand, killed," he shouted at her in English. Diana shivered and said nothing. Her mind reeled. Then, the unexpected.

CHAPTER 19

Sprawled on the gold and azure throne, the Sheik's eyes widened in surprise and his mouth fell open as he looked beyond Diana. There was the sound of the big doors closing behind her, but as the two soldiers at her side turned to see who had entered, one of them crashed to the floor with a big hairy gray beast on his back. The other soldier turned his head, to meet an iron fist that slammed against his jaw. He dropped like a rock. A strong arm encircled her waist. There was a soft kiss on the back of her neck. The deep voice that to her had to be the sweetest sound this side of heaven.

"Diana," was all he said, but it was enough.

She looked up to see the masked and hooded head towering above her. The Sheik had not moved. For there was a shining gun in the intruder's hand, pointed directly at him. The first soldier to hit the floor had quickly rolled over on his back, to see what had knocked him down. He stared with undisguised terror at the great gleaming fangs that were within inches of his face. The long gray wolfs forepaws were on his chest. He didn't move. He couldn't. His body was frozen with fear.

His arm about her waist, the Phantom walked Diana to the throne. "Get up and let a lady sit down. She's tired," he said curtly. The Sheik stared at the masked man, the gun and the big beast. He looked about wildly, mumbling. He had a thousand armed men on the palace grounds. Where were they? A strong hand grabbed his silk collar. He was lifted off the throne.

"Haven't you learned it's polite to give your seat to a lady? No manners here," said the Phantom, holding him at arm's length. He released him, and the Sheik collapsed in a heap on the floor. He huddled there, like a baby. First, that judo toss by Diana. Now this. It was too much. The Sheik did an amazing thing. He began to sob.

Diana looked at him with alarm, and despite all that had happened, felt a wave of sympathy for this man. First he sobbed. Then he cried. Then he began to howl and pound his fists on the floor. The ruler of Suda-Kalara was having a tantrum. Diana was shaken. She looked up anxiously at the Phantom. He grinned at her, a big wide grin. That reassured her.

"He's a spoiled baby. He's acting like one," he said lightly. Then his voice changed, cold as ice.

"Sit up," he commanded. The order got to the man. He sat up. There was the sound of knocking at the big closed doors, the sound of excited voices as well.

"Tell them to wait," said the Phantom.

The Sheik did as he was told. The sounds outside ceased. Then he stared up at the big stranger.

"You are the man with the dog. Mr. Walker," he said in a weak voice. He looked at the masked face for some reply. There was none. It was eerie. He couldn't see the eyes. It was like talking to a statue.

"A man like you is a disgrace to the human race," said the Phantom slowly. "We have always been burdened with tyrants. I guess we always will be."

Diana looked at him in amazement. She'd never heard him talk this way. This was not her happy, easy companion of jungle rides, Paris boulevards, midnight swims. He was remote, far away, as though speaking from a mountaintop. She realized with a shiver that this was the legendary Phantom, the Ghost Who Walks, the nemesis of evildoers everywhere.

"But I am not here to change you or your nation. That is something your own people must do. I am here to take Diana Palmer and the sacred image of the Llongo to their homes."

"Take them. Take them," said the Sheik harshly. "I never want to see them again."

"You can be sure the feeling is mutual. You know, you should be punished severely. In some places, the death penalty would not be too much for what you have done."

The Sheik stared at him fearfully. Then, surprisingly, the Phantom grinned again.

"Diana, just before I reached this room, I passed a window. I saw you in the act of throwing his Highness over your shoulder. A beautiful throw."

"Thank you," said Diana. And they both had to laugh.

"That might be a suitable punishment for his Highness," he went on. "Another demonstration like that before his troops. Willing?"

"I'd be delighted to," she said, meaning it.

"You can't," said the Sheik hoarsely. "Shoot me with that gun. I say, shoot me." He was near hysterics again.

"Don't rush us. We'll get to that," said the Phantom. Diana relaxed. He had come down from the mountain and was her good friend again.

"I said you are free to go. Take her, take that thing."

"Yes. And how far do you think we would get from this room, once we left you?"

"No, I swear, safe conduct," said the Sheik as sincerely as he could. Even Diana believed him.

But the Phantom said, "No."

"You don't accept my word? It is worth nothing to you?" said his Highness, in shocked tones.

"It is worth less than dirt. You are a criminal, a thief, a kidnapper, and the lowest of all miserable filth—a slaver," said the Phantom. And once more his voice was cold as ice and he seemed to loom like a giant over the man on the floor. The Sheik trembled and remained silent.

"Devil, bring gun," said the Phantom. Devil left the prone soldier, stepping on his face in the process, picked up the nearby rifle in his jaws and trotted to his master, laying the gun at his feet.

"You, up—open the doors."

The soldier staggered to his feet and walked weakly to the doors. They were locked from the inside. He unlocked them and swung them open. The doorway and the corridor were! filled with people packed together, soldiers, courtiers and servants. Foremost among them was Taras. All stared at their ruler lying on the floor, at the masked man, and at the girl seated on the gold and azure throne. That, in itself, was incredible. No woman had ever sat on that royal seat.

She looked at the Phantom with alarm. What could he do with all those people massed outside, through all the corridors and gardens, surrounding them on all sides? But he appeared calm, unimpressed with the mob. He reached down, grabbed the ruler by his collar and pulled him to his feet. The crowd gasped. The Sheik sagged limply. This was it. Humiliation.

"Which of you out there is in authority?" said the Phantom to the crowd. Taras stepped forward, his face showing his fear, his eyes watching the shining gun held so close to his master's head.

"I am Taras, aide to his Highness," he said in a quavering voice. He knew without being told. This was the man—the man with the dog. The Phantom—the Man Who Cannot Die. The crowds outside the chamber were buzzing. Four guards had been found in the halls, all with skull marks on their jaws, marking the progress of the stranger from the harem to the throne room. The captain of the guard's words had spread—Ghost Who Walks—sign of the Phantom.

"Taras, you will bring Loka of Llongo here at once."

Taras nodded, muttered a few words to a guard at the door who promptly disappeared.

Officers and courtiers in the halls were feverishly discussing plans to free their ruler. A sniper, a massed assault? It was too dangerous. That gun at their ruler's head.

All waited in an uneasy silence until Loka arrived. He had been found tied to a whipping post, about to be beaten. This reprieve had come at the last moment, as the jailer had raised the metal-studded whip.

Loka looked without comprehension at the scene. What had happened? They had told him nothing. There was the image, where he had left it such a short time ago. There was the ruler; there was the girl; but who was that? His stomach tightened. His heart skipped a beat. He knew instinctively, without being told.

"You are Loka?" said the Phantom, seeing the family resemblance to Lamanda Luaga. He'd seen Loka only once, in the small window of the plane at Heathrow. Loka nodded, too choked up to speak.

"You know who I am?"

Loka nodded again.

"Pick up the image, Loka."

He did as he was told, picking it up carefully and cradling it in his arms. The crowd watched tensely. By now, they all knew the legend. It was like watching a man defuse a live bomb. He was the only one who knew how to do it—but it might go off at any moment.

"When is the next international flight from this airport?" said the Phantom, directing his question to Taras. The answer involved a few moments of consultation with people in the doorway.

"There is a flight to Paris in one hour," he said.

"Reserve four seats on that plane for us. Advise me at once if they are available." The orders came out rapidly.

"Four?" said Taras, looking at the Phantom, Diana, and Loka. "Four."

"But, you—you cannot take his Highness," said Taras' anxiously. The Sheik's eyes rolled. By now he was limp and beyond caring about anything.

"It may be necessary. At once."

Taras gave an order, a man near him rushed out. They all waited in an uneasy silence. Through the windows came sounds of music and laughter from the harem. Evidently order had been restored there, and no one had told them what was going on here. It is easy to imagine what they were talking about. There was also the sound of marching feet outside—squads of soldiers moving on the gravel paths, with barked commands coming out of the night. All that power— useless to the ruler now. The man returned and nodded to Taras.

"The four seats are reserved," he said. "But his Highness?"

"His Highness will accompany us to the airport, and beyond if necessary. Now, listen to this. All of you." And he spoke in their own desert tongue. "If anyone of you makes the slightest move toward us, I will shoot his Highness. I will shoot him as dead as a cold carp." The Sheik's eyes rolled to the ceiling at this. He almost fainted. The crowd gasped at the boldness of the statement, but there were a few covered grins as well. The "cold carp" phrase was a humorous one in their language, a fact the Phantom knew. He also noticed that though they all showed expressions of proper concern for the plight of their ruler, most of them didn't appear overly worried. The exceptions were Taras and some of the courtiers and high-ranking officers who knew where their bread was buttered. For the rest, it might be said that none of them liked their cruel ruler. To the contrary, it was apparent to the sharp eyes of the Phantom that he was hated, and no greater boon could be given to these people than to turn him into a "cold carp."

"Is the Sheik's car ready?"

"His Highness's royal vehicle is waiting," said Taras bowing.

"Clear the halls," said the masked man. The halls were cleared.

They marched out of the throne room, the four of them, with Devil bringing up the rear, his eyes darting from side to side, ever alert and ready to leap if given cause. No one was anxious to give him any cause. Those jaws were terrifying. The Phantom half-walked, half-dragged the Sheik, with the gun pointed at his head. Diana clung to the Phantom's free arm. Loka followed, clutching the image, looking fearfully from side to side. And behind him, Devil. Soldiers, courtiers and servants parted—"like the Red Sea," as Diana later observed, to let them pass. All watched curiously, intrigued, amazed, with little anger. Through the rich halls, loaded with paintings, tapestries and statuary, sparkling crystal chandeliers, splashing fountains. Out onto the wide front steps where the long bubble-topped limousine waited, a chauffeur and footman in the front seat. Diana looked to one side, toward the gauzy-draped windows of the harem through which came the sounds of laughter and the tinkling of little bells.

The Phantom ordered the chauffeur and footman out of the

car. "You will drive," he told Diana. Surprised, she sat in the driver's seat. Loka sat next to her with the image on his lap. The Phantom took the Sheik into the back seat with him. As the crowds watched from every window and doorway, from all along the wide veranda, from the gardens and pathways—all the several thousand who made up this vast establishment—the car moved slowly out of the palace grounds. The gates were opened, the guards there had been advised in advance. They watched curiously as the car passed them. No vehicle of any kind followed them. That had been the Phantom's final order, and he had shaken the Sheik by the collar as he said it.

"Is that clear?" he said to one and all.

"Do everything he says," cried the frantic ruler.

So it was done that way. They reached the airport. A big plane was standing on the runway, motors idling, waiting to take off. Customs officers and airport personnel watched with wide eyes as the little procession walked through the station onto the field. At the stairs leading into the plane, a stewardess waited with a clipboard.

"Mr. Walker, party of four?" she said brightly. Then her eyes bulged as she saw the mask and the gun.

"Yes," said the Phantom.

"No, don't take me. I'll do anything you want. Give you anything you want. Just ask it—riches—whatever you ask," the Sheik pleaded, clutching the powerful arm.

"You're getting off easy. If you were a poor man, you'd spend the next twenty-five years in jail. But that's the way of the world," said his masked captor.

"You're not taking me with you?" Hope showed in his eyes. The Phantom shook his head.

"But the four seats?" said the Sheik, still unable to believe he was not going.

"The fourth seat is for Devil."

At the sound of his name, the big animal licked his hand.

"Oh, sir," said the pop-eyed stewardess, "we can't take dogs."

"We'll go into that later. Now listen to this, ruler of Suda-Kalara. I made certain preparations in case my plans didn't work like this. Tomorrow, you should receive two cables, one from the brother of your former slave, Loka." Loka, standing by the stairs with the image, was suddenly alert.

"His brother is Dr. Lamanda Luaga, President of Bangalla."

Even in his weak and battered condition, the Sheik could be amazed by that. "Luaga is his brother?"

"One of your colleagues in the Third World conclave," said the Phantom dryly.

"The Vice-President," said the Sheik faintly.

"Unless it proves necessary, he won't be told what you did

to his brother." The Sheik sighed with relief. "You will receive this cable, thanking you for finding the stolen sacred image of the Llongo, thanking you for your kindness in returning it to Bangalla in the safe care of Loka." Loka smiled for the first time in a month.

The Sheik looked worried. Even in his predicament, with a gun at his head, he could think of money. "Give it back?" he said. "But it's worth millions on the market," he said.

"So it is, but not for you," said the Phantom, looking at Diana. She shook her head. "Of all the cheap ... !" She couldn't think of a word low enough.

"You will also receive a cable from the UN Medical Delegation in Paris, advising that their junior administrator, one Diana Palmer, is visiting your kingdom on her vacation and should be given all the hospitality and courtesy for which you are so justly famous."

The Sheik stared at Diana. He didn't understand sarcasm.

"UN? You are in the UN?"

Diana froze him with a look and turned away.

A man in uniform, the copilot, appeared in the doorway of the plane above them.

"Ready for takeoff, everybody," he announced cheerfully. Diana and Loka went up the stairs, Devil remaining with his master. The copilot stared down as the Phantom started up the stairs backwards, one step at a time, his gun still pointed at the Sheik who now stood alone.

"Sir," said the copilot. "You cannot bring firearms aboard."

"He's a law enforcer," said Diana.

"Oh? Police?"

"Better than that," she said, smiling, and entered the plane.

The Phantom was halfway up the stairs when he stared up at the clouded night sky. Two jet planes roared by, high in the air. The Sheik turned to leave, but the Phantom leaped back down to the concrete and grabbed him again.

"I've changed my mind. You are going with us as far as Paris. Then we'll say good-bye."

The Sheik looked frantic again.

"I don't put it past your air force to shoot us down as soon as we get up there. With you aboard, that won't happen." And he pulled the unwilling man up the stairs into the plane.

He was quite right. That had been the hastily arranged plan, if they had boarded without the ruler. The door closed, the steps were rolled away, and the big plane took off. In the air, the jets buzzed them for a time, but on orders from the ground, held their fire.

CHAPTER 20

It was the oddest group of passengers the airline had ever carried. The Sheik sulked in his seat, refusing to open his eyes or talk to anyone. The big wolf slept on the floor at his master's feet. Black Loka clutched the shining image and refused to put it under the seat or in the locker above as they requested. The pretty girl, in her scanty harem outfit, explained that she and her masked companion had both come from a masquerade at the palace of Suda-Kalara and had made a wager they'd wear the costumes all the way to Paris. And so they did.

In Paris, there were two greeting parties, one from the Bangalla consulate to meet Loka, one from the Suda-Kalara consulate to meet the Sheik. The Bangallas escorted Loka and the image to a waiting plane, headed for his homeland. The Sheik refused to leave the plane, which was returning to Suda-Kalara. He refused to leave his seat while the maintenance crew cleaned the craft for the return trip, and was permitted to stay because he was the Sheik. He was too sunk in depression to even notice Diana and the Phantom as they left the plane. It would take him a long time to get over the events of that night in his throne room. He would have nightmares about the masked man and Diana's judo throw for months. He would endure the snickers and secret smiles of his subjects for as long as he ruled— which wasn't very long as it turned out. But that is another story.

In Paris, Diana was given a quickly arranged furlough to recover from her arduous experience. She packed another suitcase in her Paris apartment (one suitcase was lost forever in Suda-Kalara). The Phantom purchased outer clothing at an airport shop (he'd won his "wager"). With Devil, they boarded the plane that was waiting for them with Loka, to fly to Bangalla. Lamanda Luaga had arranged this special charter flight. In Mawitaan, the President himself was on hand to greet the travelers.

Flashbulbs exploded, cameras whirled, the news sped out by print and air waves. The Sacred Image of the Llongo was back again. After a brief consultation with Lamanda Luaga, Loka was sent back to his village with the image (and a squad of soldiers). There, the image was returned to its place on the altar under the leafy roof. In his own tribe, Loka did not escape punishment. After hearing his entire story, including his disgraceful spell of slavery, he was sentenced to hard labor for one year by High Chief Llionto.

It's said that with the return of the image, the legendary Llongo luck returned. Their gamblers began to win again, at the dice tables of the Blue Dragon, at the race track, at the infidel's bingo tables. Storms passed harmlessly over the village. Wild elephants no longer trampled the crops. Jungle cats no longer attacked the goat pens. Even Loka, at hard labor, got his Sala back.

The Phantom would be the last to deny the luck of the Llongo. It had washed off on him. A whole month with Diana in the Deep Woods, riding on the jungle paths, swimming in hidden jungle pools, surfing and picnicking at the Jade Hut and the golden beach at Keela-Wee. Best of all, glorious weeks at his secret Isle of Eden, romping with the animals, swimming and skiing with the dolphins (Nefertiti the beautiful, Solomon the wise.)

For all of this, he and Diana told each other, they'd have to thank the two-headed bull of the Queen of Sheba. If this isn't Llongo luck, what is?